Unbreakable

Shattered Safety Book 2

Maree Rose

Unbreakable

by Maree Rose

Blurb

Lexi's world exploded before her eyes, engulfed in a raging inferno that devoured everything she held dear.

The safe house, once a sanctuary, now lay in ruins, consumed by flames that mirrored the devastation in her heart.

Colt, Rome, Gabe, and Hunt, her protectors, swallowed by the explosion. The very men who had become her whole world ripped away in an instant.

A trusted friend's betrayal has thrust Lexi back into the clutches of the monster she had hoped to never encounter again.

Stripped of everything she held dear, she must now fight for survival in the hands of her enemy, haunted by the vision of Colt's demise.

Amidst the darkness, can she muster the strength to escape the evil from her past once more? Would the overwhelming grief of losing the men she had begun to love consume her completely?

Contents

Foreword

Hello readers!

Thank you so much for sticking with me! Even if you just want to find out what happened to Colt!

Please be aware that this duet is a reverse harem, meaning our leading lady Lexi will not have to choose between her men, because #whychoose.

There is explicit language and explicit sex scenes (a lot of them, so don't complain there is too much smut when you have been warned). This does include encounters with more than one of her men at one time. This is absolutely an adult romance and is intended for readers 18+ due to the language and content. Our heroes can dirty talk with the best of them... and this does include a touch of degradation.

This book is darker than the first one in the duet. There are a few more triggers in this than there were in the previous ones. You will read about new and very nasty evil characters. There are mentions of past trauma, past attempts of murder, past child abuse, and past abuse of lethal skill, these have impacted the characters within the story giving rise to PTSD. There is also on-page violence, abuse, and torture. If any of these things are triggering for you please do not read this story.

Thank you and I hope that you enjoy Unbreakable.

PS. Mum, please, I'm still begging you NOT TO READ THESE BOOKS! But since I know you're going to ignore the warning, we are never going to speak of what you read in here...

To those who complained
the first book had too much smut...
This book is not for you...
But thank you for inspiring me to add even more.

Chapter 1

Alexis

24 HRS SINCE EXPLOSION

It was not every day you woke up chained to a wall. But considering the man that sat casually in the chair facing me, it didn't really surprise me that I was. The large sharp looking knife he was inspecting in his hand didn't surprise me either.

He was a good looking man, very typical Italian looking with short black hair and a maintained beard framing high cheekbones and dark eyes. Unfortunately, I knew the monster hiding beneath that good looking face.

The cold metal around my wrists cut into my skin as it held me chained against the brick wall with my arms stretched out above my head to form a Y.

The room was a bare cell with brick walls. It reminded me strongly of a dark, dank dungeon in old castles. I could even see water trailing down the two corners of the room. I could see where they created damp puddles on the concrete floor. There was a threadbare mattress against one wall–that I'm sure would also be damp with how close to the water it was–plus a toilet that seemed to have been installed recently.

Two years ago, I would have been screaming and panicking to find myself waking up in this position. But I was no longer that person. And the very clear memories of watching Colt being shot, and the house with the men I had been falling for being blown up, had nothing but rage burning in my blood.

As I surveyed the room, I noticed the flickering light bulb hanging from the ceiling, casting an eerie yellow glow across the walls. The air was thick with the musty smell of dampness and neglect, mixed with the metallic scent of blood that lingered in the air.

I could feel my heart pounding in my chest, but I refused to let fear take over. I knew that showing any weakness in front of this man would only give him the upper hand. Instead, I stared him down with as much defiance as I could muster, trying to hide the fact that my wrists were starting to ache from the chains.

The man across from me wore a cruel smirk, his eyes glinting with malice as he twirled the knife in his hand. The dim light in the bare brick cell made the blade glimmer menacingly. "For so long I thought you were going to be the empress to my empire. Imagine my surprise when you betrayed me."

I didn't respond. I simply glared at him with hatred, my jaw clenched tight.The cold metal of the chains was cutting into my wrists as I strained against them. Surprise flickered briefly in his eyes, as if he didn't expect me to possess such a fierce spirit.

"I counted every day I was in that prison cell and marked it with thoughts of revenge at your betrayal," he continued, his voice laced with venom. I could hear the evil in his tone now, the darkness lurking beneath his handsome façade.

"Somehow, I think the attempted murder warranted a little betrayal," I retorted, my voice shaking slightly with anger.

He scoffed and stood up, unfolding himself from the chair as he began to stalk towards me. "I guess, I only have myself to blame for thinking that with the number of times I thrust my knife into your beautiful chest, you would have done me the courtesy of dying."

I didn't flinch, meeting his gaze with defiance. "I guess your aim was a little off," I shot back, inwardly berating myself for taunting a madman.

"Well, we'll try not to make that mistake again this time when I've finished with you," he said, a cold smirk playing at the corners of his lips.

"Someone will find me," I said, desperately trying to cling to hope.

"Really? Who? Your protectors are dead. Ash in the wind," he sneered.

The weight of his words hit me like a ton of bricks, and I had to swallow down the sob that rose in my throat. "You're a wanted man," I said, my voice barely above a whisper. "Someone will find you to put you behind bars again."

He stood there with a menacing look on his face as the cold metal of the knife grazed against my skin, tracing a line from the hollow of my throat to the top of my shirt. The chill that ran down my spine made me tremble ever so slightly, and I couldn't help but feel a sense of dread wash over me. His chuckle was dark, and it echoed around the room like a bad omen.

"I've learned from my previous mistakes. They won't find me, therefore they won't find you. No one is coming to save you. You're mine to do anything I want," he said, his voice dripping with malice and hatred.

As he spoke, his eyes never left the tip of the knife as it traced against my skin, and he seemed to be lost in some dark obsession. "You've heard of a death by a thousand cuts, right?" he asked, not even waiting for my response. "I know it wasn't really a thousand days since your betrayal, but what're a few hundred extra cuts to prove a point, right? And it won't be all at once, just one a day. I feel there is a sense of fairness in that."

I gritted my teeth, unable to hide my anger and disgust. "How considerate of you," I replied sarcastically, my voice laced with venom.

He chuckled again, relishing in his own twisted sense of humor, before he dragged the knife down the front of my shirt, parting the material as if it was butter, and letting the two halves fall loose. He used the tip of the knife to brush them away, exposing my bare breasts to him. I regretted my decision not to wear a bra while I was at the safe house, but I knew it would have just been something more for him to cut through.

With his free hand, he trailed a finger along some of the scars that he had inflicted, his focus completely on my chest. Then he grabbed one of my breasts and squeezed it to an almost painful degree. I tried to swallow my whimper, but the memory of the last men to touch me where he was now made it impossible.

"I actually missed these," he growled, before moving his hand to my other breast and squeezing again. "Maybe once I'm done, I'll cut them off and mount them on my wall like a trophy."

I couldn't stop the shudder that went through me as I felt him touch me like that, with his breath so close to my skin. He continued to fondle me aggressively, and I felt sick to my stomach.

"Your mind will break long before your body does," he said almost thoughtfully, his attention still on his hand. "Maybe once I've broken your mind, I'll have you ride my cock again like a good little pet."

Just the thought made my nausea return, and I couldn't hold back my response. "The moment you release my hands, I'll cut off your cock and feed it to you," I spat.

His eyes flicked up to mine again, and for a moment, I stopped paying attention to what was more important. I didn't even register that he had moved his other hand; it happened so quickly. It even took a moment for the pain to register in my mind before I felt the blazing fire along my left ribs below my breast. The pain screamed into my mind, and I jerked against the chain as he took a step away from me and brought the knife up between us.

There was blood glistening against the metal blade. Droplets slid down towards the handle to glow starkly against the pale skin of his fingers. My blood.

He turned the knife in front of him as though admiring the color that slowly dripped from the blade while I swallowed down the scream at the back of my throat behind a clenched jaw. Tears came to my eyes that I rapidly blinked away. I would not show my fear and pain to this monster. He did not deserve anything from me.

His eyes lifted back to mine as he raised the knife to his mouth and ran his tongue along the blade, my blood smearing in a vibrant red slash across his mouth.

He dropped his hand with the knife back down to his side as he smirked at me. "We'll see how long you keep that cute new backbone you have grown. I missed the sound of your screams, Fiore Mio."

The nickname he used to call me on his lips made a shudder move along my spine and I had to forcefully swallow down the vomit that crept up my throat. But he chose that moment to turn from me, pick up the chair and exit the room via a door I hadn't seen before. I glimpsed stairs beyond the door seconds before he slammed it shut with a metal on metal thud, the lock sounding loud in the silence. And then he turned off the lights, plunging me into cold darkness.

Out of everything he had done since I opened my eyes, that was the worst.

Chapter 2

Rome

29 HRS SINCE EXPLOSION

I despised hospitals. The strong odors of industrial cleaners and disease lingered in the air, causing memories of my childhood visits to emergency rooms to flood my mind. The beeping of machines only added to the sense of discomfort and unease that had settled over me. The man pacing back and forth only worsened the situation, as his frenzied movements left a visible path on the linoleum floor.

I felt frustrated and on edge, and I couldn't help but snap at him. "Sit down," I said sharply. "The doctor still needs to clear you and Hunt before you can leave."

But my words fell on deaf ears. Colt gave me a withering glare and continued to pace. "I won't settle down until our girl is back in our arms where she belongs," he declared. "It's already been over twenty-four hours."

I couldn't argue with him. I shared his burning desire to be reunited with Lexi, and my own emotions were running high. So, I turned my attention to the computer in front of me, determined to locate her.

Despite my frustration with Colt's pacing, I knew that arguing with him was pointless. He was recovering from internal bruising and extensive external bruising and cuts from a bullet to his vest and a subsequent fall through a dining table, but nothing could keep him still until we found Lexi.

Colt paused his restless pacing and turned to me, his eyes burning with impatience. "Where are they, Rome? And why isn't Kacey answering my calls?" he demanded.

I gave him a dry look, hiding the stress that was churning inside me. "If I could have miraculously pulled a location out of my ass, don't you think I would have done that in the last two weeks that I was trying to find Dominick?" I retorted sharply. "As for Kacey, I have no clue. Maybe try calling him for the hundredth time."

He growled in frustration and resumed pacing as he dialed Kacey's number once again. I didn't expect much to come of it, but the moment Kacey picked up the phone, Colt's pacing abruptly stopped and he snarled into the receiver.

"Shut the fuck up, Dominick has Lexi," he spat, his expression contorted with rage. It was a look that would have frightened anyone else, but I knew him too well. I knew that same feeling of fury and desperation.

"You think I let him take her? We barely made it out alive, so don't you dare talk like that right now," Colt barked back, his voice laced with anger.

In reality, we had Gabe to thank for our survival. He had spotted the explosives just in time for us to drag an unconscious Colt and Sam to safety in the pool at the back of the house, watching the world explode from under the water. I had received an alert that someone matching Sam's son Nathan's description had been dropped off at the hospital, but I had yet to speak with the still-unconscious Sam.

Colt growled into the phone once more. "I don't give a fuck what you think, Kacey. Get your ass in a car and head to this address yesterday." He snapped his fingers at me, but I had already been paying attention to the conversation and quickly rattled off the address of a nearby warehouse that we had set up for him to repeat to Kacey before hanging up.

Colt's frustration was palpable, and I could tell he was on the verge of hurling his phone against the wall. However, the sound of the door opening brought a sudden halt to his actions, and we both turned to see Gabe and Hunt entering the room.

Gabe slumped into the chair beside me, his weary expression mirroring the exhaustion that I felt. Hunt stood leaning against the wall, and I could see the tension etched on his face, betraying the pain he was hiding.

Colt's gaze shifted towards Hunt, and he asked, "How's the arm?"

Hunt lifted his arm away from his body, and I could see the bandage wrapped around his upper arm. "Stitches. I'm fine," he replied, his voice tight with pain.

The deep bullet graze on his arm was a testament to how close he had come to losing his life. He had his arms raised at the time, and the bullet had missed his head by mere inches.

Colt just frowned in response, the worry etched on his face. We were all exhausted and battered, physically and emotionally, but we couldn't afford to give up. We needed to find Lexi, no matter what.

"Sam's awake," Gabe grunted from beside me and Colt's eyes immediately swung to him. Seconds later he was marching through the open door on his way to hunt her down.

I was right behind him, my laptop now closed and under my arm, as I snarled at Colt's back. "You're meant to wait for the doctor to be discharged."

He flicked his angry gaze over his shoulder to me before he responded. "And chance her disappearing before she explains what the fuck she did and what she knows? No, not happening. The doctor can catch up."

There was no stopping him. If anything I could see people in the corridor subtly moving out of his way as he stormed towards his destination.

I heard Sam's sob as I followed Colt into her room and saw her clutching desperately at her son in her arms. I could see the scrapes and bruises that had been left on her by our girl and I felt a quick rush of pride at how she had handled Sam. Nathan thankfully appeared completely uninjured from his ordeal.

Sam's tearful voice broke the silence, "Please, please don't hurt me. I swear I didn't want to do anything, but they had my Nathan."

Colt let out a low growl, and Sam's sobs grew louder, causing Nathan to start crying in her arms. It was a painful sound, one that hit me in the gut. I watched as Colt tried to swallow down whatever he was about to say before asking, "How long? Do you know where he took her?"

Sam shook her head before he even finished speaking. "They took Nathan the afternoon before. I don't know how they knew about me, but I think they followed me because they knew where I left my son each day while I worked. They told me they would kill him if I didn't let them inside, but I could only get in at certain times, so they held me until I could let them in. I'm so sorry."

I gently squeezed Colt's shoulder, trying to calm him down before he could lash out at her. "Where did they hold you?" I asked as gently as possible.

Sam cringed, and I knew her answer was going to disappoint us. "I don't know. They kept something over my head when they took me there, and when they dragged me back to the house."

As Colt clenched his fists, I could see the anger building in his eyes. But I knew that lashing out at Sam wouldn't solve anything. Instead, I focused on getting more information from her.

"Okay, don't worry about it," I said, trying to reassure her. "Can you tell us anything else about what happened? Did you see or hear anything that could help us find Lexi?"

Sam shook her head, her eyes filled with tears. "I'm sorry, I didn't see or hear anything. They kept me in the dark the whole time."

Colt let out another growl as he turned and stormed out of the hospital room, barking orders. "Get me discharged right now, and find out how close our friends are."

Letting Gabe and Hunt follow after him, I went in search of the doctor to get us out of there.

Chapter 3

Alexis

34 HRS SINCE EXPLOSION

I wasn't sure how long I had been in the dark before the light came on again. It could have been hours or days for all I knew. But given Nick's promise to cut me each day, I could rule out the latter.

The pain from the cut had thankfully reduced to only a dull throb.

Thoughts of the men who stole my heart tried to creep into my mind before I shut the door on them. I couldn't afford to let myself fall apart whilst I was here. I couldn't allow myself to grieve for what I lost just yet.

As the door opened, I expected to see Nick again to taunt me but I was surprised to see two women enter the room. One was carrying what appeared to be medical supplies while another carried some food and water.

They both had pale skin and different shades of brown hair tied back from their faces. Bruises littered the skin I could see around the plain black shapeless dresses they wore.

Their eyes were downturned as they made their way slowly into the room and over to me. Neither let me down from the chains.

As the one with medical supplies started working on the cut at my side the other slowly started to try to feed me by hand.

I didn't trust the food and water. I had learned not to trust anything given to me by those I didn't trust, as it could be laced with something that could knock me out or make me more susceptible to their manipulations. So, I tried to resist their attempts to feed me.

However, the woman with the food persisted, urging me to eat something. "You need to keep your strength up," she said softly, her voice full of concern.

I remained silent, but she continued to coax me, offering me small bites of bread and sips of water. I was thirsty and hungry, but I couldn't bring myself to trust anything they gave me.

Meanwhile, the other woman was working on my wound, cleaning and dressing it with expert precision. I winced as she probed the cut, but I didn't make a sound. She politely pulled the two halves of the shirt together and tied them together as best she could to offer me some sense of modesty.

As she finished up, she turned to me and spoke for the first time. "I'm sorry we have to do this," she said, her voice barely above a whisper. "We're just following orders."

I looked at her and I could see the fear in her eyes. "Help me. Please help me escape from here," I pleaded softly.

She was already shaking her head vigorously. "They would kill us."

"Please." My volume increased as I begged her.

A chuckle came from the door and for a moment I thought it was Nick, but when I looked in that direction, I saw it was the mountain of a man that grabbed me from the safe house. Now that I was looking at him more clearly, I vaguely recognized him as one of the men who worked for Nick prior to him going to prison.

I was surprised I hadn't made the connection before, but then Nick did always like to surround himself with overly muscled idiots so it was easy to dismiss the similarities. His dark hair was cut short but still allowed for curls to form. It looked wet but in an overly gelled way. His brown eyes were nothing but evil as he watched from the doorway.

"I wouldn't bother trying. I should thank you, really. Before you betrayed him, Nick was going soft; he even implemented a no touching rule with the women." He slowly walked into the room and came to stand behind the woman I was speaking to before he grabbed her roughly around the nape of her neck, shaking her almost like a ragdoll before dragging her back against his front, his other hand coming around to wrap around her throat before he licks the side of her face disgustingly.

I watched as she flinched and shuddered in his hold, tears slowly trailing down her cheeks, before he continued. "Now though, I can use this pretty little cunt however I want. The more she talks to you and doesn't silently do as she is told, like the mouse she is meant to be, the more painful I will make it for her."

I felt a wave of disgust and anger wash over me at the man's words and actions. This was the kind of sick, twisted behavior that Nick and his people engaged in, and it made my blood boil.

But I couldn't let my emotions get the better of me. I needed to stay calm and think of a way out of there.

I turned my attention back to the woman, who was now trembling in the man's grasp. "I'm sorry," I said softly, trying to reassure her. "I won't put you in any more danger."

The man laughed again, tightening his grip on the woman's throat. "Oh, don't worry about her. She's used to it by now."

I could see the fear in her watery blue eyes and knew that he was lying. No one could get used to being treated like that.

I felt a surge of anger at the man, but I knew that I needed to keep my cool if I was going to get out of there alive. I needed to find a way to escape and take this woman with me.

As the man continued to gloat, I scanned the room for any possible escape routes. I couldn't see anything that could help us, but I knew that I had to keep looking.

Meanwhile, the woman continued to tremble in his grasp. I needed to find a way to get her out of here and away from these monsters.

I looked up at the man and spoke with as much confidence as I could muster. "You may think you have all the power here, but you're wrong. I will find a way out of this place, and when I do, I will make sure you pay for what you've done to me and to these women."

The man laughed, his grip on the woman tightening. "You're in no position to make threats, little girl," he sneered.

But I didn't back down. I knew that I had to show him that I was not afraid of him, even if I was terrified inside. "You will regret underestimating me," I said firmly, hoping that my words would somehow give me strength.

He just laughed in response before turning and shoving the woman back out the door, the other woman scampering out after her as the man turned back to me. He reached up and released each of my hands and let me drop unaided to the floor, the impact jarring my knees.

"Be thankful he said you're off limits. You have ten minutes before the lights go out again," he said to me as he turned and walked back out the door, closing it with a clang of metal.

I sat on the cold, hard ground, my hands still numb from being chained for so long. The woman's pleading eyes haunted me, and I felt a pang of guilt for putting her in danger. But I couldn't give up on escaping. I needed to keep fighting.

I tried to stand up, but my legs gave out from under me, and I fell back down onto the floor. I groaned in pain, my whole body aching from the constant abuse it had endured.

I looked around the small, dimly lit room, trying to find anything that could help me escape. But there was nothing. No windows, no doors except for the one that the man had just left through.

I sighed, resigned to the fact that I was stuck here for the time being. At least the man had said I was off-limits, which meant I didn't have to worry about him hurting me. But the thought of being trapped in the dark again was overwhelming.

I slowly crawled over to the toilet and pulled myself up and used it before stumbling back over to the mattress. I was thankful it wasn't as damp as I thought it might be, but I still dragged it away from the wall as best I could.

It hadn't been ten minutes when the lights went off, catching me off guard. I knew I shouldn't have expected any better from the ruthless criminals who had taken me captive. Time seemed to crawl by agonizingly slowly in the pitch darkness. Without any external light source, I was completely disoriented, unable to tell whether it was day or night.

Chapter 4

Colt

35 HRS SINCE EXPLOSION

The pain I was in was indescribable. And I wasn't even talking about the extensive bruising. The pain of having Lexi taken from us squeezed my heart. The rage I felt at those who took her burned inside me like an inferno.

Instead of pacing around the sterile hospital room like a caged animal, I was now pacing the cold, empty floor of a warehouse, waiting impatiently for Kacey to arrive. Every second felt like an eternity, and I couldn't shake off the overwhelming sense of helplessness that was weighing me down. The longer we waited, the more I feared for Lexi's safety, and the stronger my rage burned.

I clenched my fists, feeling it boiling inside me. The memory of Lexi's laughter and her warm hugs flashed before my eyes, making me feel even more determined to find her and bring her back home.

Rome was once again in a chair at the side of the room splitting his attention between his computer and me pacing the room. "Kacey's pulling in now," he announced after I assumed he opened the warehouse door for Kacey's car.

I came to a standstill and waited for Kacey to make his way into the room. His footsteps were loud in the silence as he made his way towards us. He stormed into the room like a thundercloud with Gabe and Hunt following closely behind him.

"How could you let him get to her? I trusted you to keep her safe!" he yelled as he stormed towards me. I was on him in seconds, my hand wrapped around his throat and his back slamming into the wall.

"How the fuck did he know we even had her? You were meant to get rid of your leaks," I snarled into his face.

We both stood there practically growling at each other before the silence was suddenly broken.

"Where the fuck is my best friend you useless piece of shit."

The tiny package of blond hair and muscles that stormed into the room had me choking and releasing the hold I had on Kacey's throat.

"Ashley?" I sputtered in astonishment.

She paused to look at me and flashed me a grin. "Oh hey, Colten, long time and all that."

I was still gaping at her. "What the hell are you doing here?"

"Trying to find out why that asshole isn't looking for my best friend who disappeared under his watch."

I frowned before the pieces suddenly fell into place. "I knew the voice on the messages was familiar."

She frowned at me. "What messages? Are you talking about my messages to Lexi? Where the fuck is she?" She became increasingly agitated the more she spoke, fisting her hands on her hips and turning her ire directly toward me.

Rome suddenly raised a hand to interrupt. "Ah, how the hell did you get in without me seeing you and allowing you access."

She flashed him a grin. "I stowed away in his trunk. I thought he was finally going to find my best friend." She shot another glare toward Kacey.

I held up my hands. I was so confused and everything seemed to be going in a million directions. "You're Lexi's best friend? The one who taught her how to shoot?"

She frowned at me again. "Yes. How do you even know her?"

I rubbed my temples, the headache already creeping in. "Lexi has been with us the last two weeks."

She frowned further. "So where is she now? Is she somewhere safe?"

"No, what do you know about Lexi's situation?" I asked as I winced at her questions.

She flinched and I knew that look on her, "You know I'm not meant to know anything."

I gave her a dry look. "And I know that wouldn't stop you."

She just shrugged as she raised an eyebrow at me. "Your point?"

"Dominick abducted her from the safe house last night." The drain of color from her face told me she knew everything.

"Umm, how exactly do you know this crazy bitch?" Kacey snarked from against the wall where he hadn't moved after Ashley came in.

She shot him a glare and growled in his direction. But I just laughed.

"Everyone, this is Ashley. Apparently, she is Lexi's best friend. But she is also my sister."

She saluted in the direction of Rome, Gabe, and Hunt before turning her hand and flipping Kacey the bird, to which he rolled his eyes.

I heard a noise from Rome's direction to see him doing something with his phone before he looked directly at me. "Our friends are here."

I looked back toward Ashley with a grimace. "Fuck. This is not going to end well."

I heard the sound of a motorcycle along with a vehicle pulling into the warehouse as Ashley's eyes widened. I gave her a look as I started to follow the others out into the warehouse area but she grabbed my arm to stop me as I went to pass her.

"You called them? Why did you call them?" she hissed at me.

I couldn't help the anger that flashed through me at her stubbornness. "Just because you stopped talking to them, doesn't mean I did too. I am desperate. I can't get her back alone, I need their help. And I would do just about anything to get her back with us, I don't care how you feel about it."

I saw it dawn on her as a small smile tugged at her lips and a softness entered her face. "You love her, don't you?"

I wrenched my arm out of her grip and proceeded through the door. There was no way I was going to even look at my feelings before I got Lexi back.

The group of men that had entered were all greeting Rome, Gabe, and Hunt and being introduced to Kacey as I made my way into the space. There were three new people there, the biggest was in the process of laying a motorcycle jacket over the back of a Harley Davidson while his attention was on the others giving greetings. His long brown hair was pulled into a messy ponytail and I could see that too much time outdoors was starting to bleach it a blond color, yet the full facial hair was still a deep brown and longer than last time I saw him. Tattoos covered his body from his neck down and he looked like he had enough muscle to lift the motorcycle he was standing next to.

The second man was smaller, but no less tattooed and only slightly less bulky. His hair was shorter, but still longer than average. From this distance, his hair looked black but I knew it was just a very dark brown. The waves were starting to make his hair look almost stylishly untidy. He too had what looked like several days of growth on his face but it was much more maintained.

The last of the group was just as tall but had more of a swimmer's body and only a few tattoos could be seen on his arms. His blond hair was short at the sides but long on the top, as long as Hunt's, but was completely straight. His clean shaven face only made the grin he wore seem wider as he tucked his aviators into the top of his shirt.

My attention returned to the first man to see he had turned towards us, but it wasn't me he was looking at and I turned to take in the trainwreck I knew was about to happen.

"Mon Ange," he breathed out, his attention solely on Ash.

She looked like she had taken a punch to her chest as she forced a slow breath out. "Nix," she responded stubbornly.

He scoffed at her. "That wasn't what you used to call me."

She narrowed her eyes at him and tilted her head. "Yes, well, there is a lot I don't do anymore."

He shook his head in response and turned his blue eyes towards me. "Brother," he said simply and walked over to clasp my arm and draw me into a back slapping hug.

The others also moved to do the same as Kacey looked at me curiously.

"These are my foster brothers, Phoenix, Beckett, and Maverick. But the rest of the world knows them as the Black Wolves," I explained.

I saw Ash flinch at the name and wondered if she had even heard it before.

Kacey turned on me, his eyes wide and anger crossing his face. "Are you fucking kidding me? You brought a group of wanted criminals to a meeting with a US Marshal?"

Rage washed through me and must have shown on my face because Kacey took an involuntary step backward as I pointed at him. "If you keep going I'll shoot you myself and forget about involving you in our search for Lexi."

He raised his hands in a placating gesture and said, "You know how much she meant to me. I want her safe almost as much as you. Let's just pretend I've left my badge at the door then shall we?"

I took a deep breath, trying to control my anger. "Fine," I said through gritted teeth. "Let's focus on finding Lexi and forget about who we bring to meetings."

Kacey nodded and the tension in the room eased slightly.

I turned to everyone else and motioned towards the room I had just exited. "Let's go sit down so we can go over what we do know before we start working on what we don't."

Lexi was out there somewhere, and we were going to find her, no matter what it took.

Chapter 5

Alexis

49 HRS SINCE EXPLOSION

The frigid temperature of the concrete floor had penetrated my very being, infiltrating even through the flimsy barrier of the threadbare mattress beneath me. Despite my best efforts to stay awake, I repeatedly fell asleep only to startle myself awake, unable to shake off the numbing sensation that consumed my body. Time seemed to have lost all meaning in the oppressive darkness, each passing second felt like a never-ending hour.

After so long in the persistent dark the light coming back on was startling as was the metal clang of the opening door.

The nameless goon from my previous encounter strolled leisurely into the room, his demeanor exuding a sense of twisted pleasure as he approached my huddled figure, tightly curled up on the decrepit mattress. In one swift motion, he yanked me up by my arms, and I was unable to contain the small whimper that escaped my lips as he dragged me toward the wall to re-shackle my arms. He let out a chuckle of sadistic satisfaction, taking delight in my momentary lapse of composure.

After completing his task, he retreated through the door silently again, leaving behind a void that was quickly filled by the grinning visage of Nick. Anticipating the worst, I braced myself for the impending confrontation. I was well aware of what his return signified, but at least his presence acted as a sort of internal timer.

Nick wasted no time in unleashing his verbal onslaught, relishing in the discomfort he caused me. "I've heard that Enzo had a lot of fun last night, all thanks to you," he taunted, the malicious glint in his eyes belying his amusement.

The name Enzo was a perfect fit for the brutish thug, complete with all the stereotypical hallmarks of an overbearing Italian bully. The mere mention of his name caused a shudder to run down my spine, and I felt my blood boiling with rage.

Despite my best efforts, my voice quivered with emotion as I spat out my response. "He's not welcome," I hissed, gritting my teeth.

Nick's laughter filled the air, an audible manifestation of his twisted pleasure at my misery. His gaze roamed over my body, taking in every single wound and abrasion, like a predator assessing its prey. I felt exposed and vulnerable, as if I were nothing more than a piece of meat on display, ready to be devoured at any moment.

With a languid movement, he traced the outline of my collarbone with his finger before gliding it slowly down the length of my body. His gaze followed his finger's path. "I must say," he remarked, "I do like the alterations you've made to your physique." It was almost taunting, the way he reveled in my appearance.

As his touch lingered on my skin, I recoiled, feeling violated by his actions. But he didn't seem to notice, too busy reveling in his power over me. The smug grin on his face only grew wider as he pressed his fingers hard against the dressing over the wound he'd inflicted on me last time and I couldn't restrain the whimper that escaped me.

"It's a shame, really," he said, his voice dripping with sarcasm. "I almost regret having to keep you locked up like this. Almost."

He reached out again, grabbing my chin with a force that made me wince. His grip was unyielding as he forced me to look up at him. I tried to pull away, but his grasp only tightened, making me feel like I was suffocating under his hold.

"But then I remember why you're here," he continued, a gleeful light in his eyes. "You thought you could betray me and get away with it. How foolish of you. And now, look at you."

I felt sick to my stomach at the thought of what he was going to do to me. Every fiber of my being screamed at me to fight back, but I knew it was pointless. I was trapped, at his mercy, and there was nothing I could do to escape him.

He leaned in, his breath hot against my ear, and whispered, "I'm going to enjoy each time I come in here to remind you of the consequences of betraying me. And believe me, Fiore Mio, the punishment will be much worse than anything you've experienced so far."

I glared at him, my anger simmering just beneath the surface. "Oh, is that what you're calling it? Betrayal? I thought it was more like escaping the clutches of a sociopath."

Nick's grip on my chin tightened, digging into my jaw bone. "Watch your tongue, Fiore Mio," he growled.

I could feel my heart racing as Nick's grip on my chin tightened. I knew I had to be careful with my words, but I couldn't help but feel the anger boiling inside me.

"Or what?" I challenged him. "You'll hurt me more? Lock me up tighter? You already took everything away from me, what more could you possibly do?"

Nick's smirk turned into a cruel grin, revealing his sharp teeth. "Oh, there's always something more I can do," he said, his voice laced with malice.

He released my chin and walked around the small cell, his eyes never leaving mine. I felt a shiver run down my spine as he circled me like a predator sizing up its prey.

"Perhaps I'll bring in some of my men to have some fun with you," he mused, his voice low and dangerous. "Or maybe I'll just leave you alone in the dark for a few days."

I gritted my teeth, refusing to show him any fear, or how much his words affected me. "You're a monster," I spat out, my voice trembling with anger.

Nick laughed, his eyes glittering with amusement. "Oh, you have no idea, Fiore Mio," he said, his Italian accent thickening. "But you'll learn. You'll learn that no one crosses me and lives to tell the tale."

I rolled my eyes, refusing to give him the satisfaction of seeing me cower. "You sound like a bad mafia movie," I retorted, my voice dripping with sarcasm. "What's next? Are you going to make me an offer I can't refuse?"

Nick's face darkened, his amusement turning to rage. "You think this is a joke?" he snarled, taking a step closer to me.

"No," I said, holding my ground. "I think you're a pathetic excuse for a man who gets off on hurting others."

A flicker of anger flashed across Nick's face before he composed himself. "Don't test me. You know what I'm capable of."

"I do," I agreed. "And that's why I'll never stop fighting you. Even if you kill me, I know someone will come after you. Someone who will make sure justice is served."

Nick chuckled darkly. "You really think anyone cares about a nobody like you? You're disposable, easily replaced."

"Maybe," I said with a tilt of my head. "But even if I am forgotten, I'll die knowing I never gave up. That I never let you break me completely."

Nick leaned in close to my ear and whispered, "You're not as strong as you think you are. And I will break you. Don't even bother thinking about escape either. No matter where you go, no matter where you try to hide, I will always find you."

I closed my eyes, trying to block out his words, but they echoed in my mind, taunting me.

He took the opportunity to wrap his hand around the front of my throat and jaw, squeezing painfully. But it was still nothing on the pain that shot through me as he sliced his knife across my right ribs.

It's deeper than the last one and actually drew a gasp from me. Nick took advantage and slammed his mouth against mine, biting hard into my lip before his tongue swept into my mouth briefly and then retreated before I had the chance to react.

I could taste the metallic tang of blood in my mouth and felt the warm trickle of blood running down my side.

I could feel the darkness creeping in at the edges of my vision, and I knew I needed to fight to stay conscious. I didn't know what he would do if I lost consciousness.

I must have made some sound as he pulled back, a wicked grin on his face. "That's the sound I like to hear, my dear. Pain suits you much better than defiance."

I gritted my teeth and tried to suppress the tears that threatened to spill over. I refused to give him the satisfaction.

Nick leaned in close again, his breath hot against my ear. "Remember, Fiore Mio, you brought this on yourself. All you had to do was stay loyal to me."

As Nick turned to leave, I took a deep breath and spoke up, my voice hoarse from the pressure on my throat. "You can hurt me all you want, Nick, but you'll never break me."

Nick paused with his back to me. "We'll see about that," he said quietly, before walking out of the room and slamming the door behind him. The room plunged into darkness once more.

Alone again, I closed my eyes and focused on my breathing, trying to ignore the pain and the fear. I knew I'd have to keep fighting, to never give up hope of escape. And maybe, just maybe, I would be able to bring Nick to justice for all the pain he had caused me and others like me.

Chapter 6

Hunt

51 HRS SINCE EXPLOSION

My growing exasperation at the lack of progress was taking a toll on my mental state, pushing me to the brink of insanity.

All I could think about was the urgent need to bring our girl back to her rightful place, away from the clutches of that asshole Dominick. As each moment passed, my anxiety for her safety intensified.

Rome, an exceptional hacker with impressive skills, had already dedicated two whole weeks to locating his whereabouts. However, despite the addition of Beckett, an even more proficient hacker, our efforts seemed to be leading us nowhere. We were encountering obstacle after obstacle, hitting blank walls with each passing hour.

Meanwhile, Ash seemed to derive a perverse pleasure from taunting Kacey with her biting tongue, all while she steadfastly refused to acknowledge the presence of her foster brothers. It was patently evident that a significant backstory lay beneath Ash's peculiar behavior, but my thoughts were so wholly consumed by the safety and well-being of Lexi that I could scarcely divert my attention elsewhere.

Suddenly, Rome let out a resounding whistle, which echoed throughout the room, causing everyone to abruptly turn their heads toward the source of the sound. He was pointing towards the colossal TV that had previously been displaying various boxes of inconsequential search results. The screen was now showing vivid and detailed images of two men, which immediately caught everyone's attention.

Colt and Nix strolled over to the screen, examining the images with great interest. "Marcus Stine," Rome began and looked towards Kacey. "One of the names I revealed to you as a traitor in your department. I know you have already eliminated the leak, but he is still receiving deposits, which suggests that he is still working for the person who was paying him."

Kacey narrowed his eyes at the image displayed on the screen, his expression becoming increasingly severe. "I'll go and retrieve him, and bring him here," he announced with a determined tone.

Nix looked at Kacey carefully, his eyes assessing him. "Take Rick and Hunt with you," he commanded. Kacey frowned and looked towards Rick who just grinned at him and shot him a wink.

Kacey looked back to Nix and acknowledged his instructions with a nod, while Colt moved closer to the screen, observing the other man's image more closely. "I recognize this bastard from the safe house," he declared with disdain. "Enzo Corletti. That son of a bitch was the one who snatched Lexi. Nix and I will go after him," he announced with a firm determination in his voice.

Nix nodded in agreement with Colt's plan, his own eyes flashing with determination. "We'll need to move quickly," he said, his voice low and urgent. "They won't stay in one place for long, and we can't risk losing them again."

I moved to stand with Rick while we waited for Kacey. We stood silently, watching as Kacey retrieved the necessary information to track down Stine. The tension in the room was palpable as everyone focused on their respective tasks, all working towards the common goal of rescuing Lexi.

Finally, Kacey spoke up as he moved towards us, his voice steady and resolute. "I've got the location," he announced, holding up his phone to display the address. "Let's move out."

Rick chuckled and threw an arm around Kacey's shoulder. "Come on then Detective Douche, let's move out."

Kacey growled at him and threw his arm off as we made our way towards Kacey's vehicle to move on Stine's location, while Nix and Colt set off in pursuit of Corletti.

It was a long drive that took three and a half hours, and as we drove towards Stine's location, Kacey briefed us on the plan. "We need to approach cautiously," he said, his eyes fixed on the road ahead. "Stine is a slippery asshole with the training to be a US Marshal, and we can't afford to let him slip through our fingers."

Rick, who was slumped in the front seat watching Kacey just grinned. "I hope you're not stating the obvious, Kace, because I thought that's why we're all here," he quipped, his tone dripping with sarcasm.

Kacey shot him a withering look before continuing, "We need to be prepared for anything. Stine may have backup, and we can't underestimate him."

I couldn't help but chuckle at Rick's sass, earning a grin from him in response. It was moments like these that helped ease the tension and reminded us that even in the face of danger, we could still find humor.

As we approached the location, Kacey slowed the vehicle and pulled up outside a run-down house. Kacey motioned for us to follow him as he made his way up the long walkway towards the entrance, his hand resting on the gun holstered at his waist.

I heard Rick quip to Kacey. "So have you ever been fucked over by a criminal Kacey? Or maybe the more important question is have you ever been fucked by a criminal?"

Kacey stumbled on the footpath and his steps faltered as he looked at Rick. "Really? Do you feel that now is the time to ask that? Stine probably heard you."

"Yeah, I already clocked him trying to escape out the back door. I figured I'd give him a little head start just to make it more fun." Rick said with a grin.

Kacey stopped walking, making Rick run into the back of him. Rick's hands gripped Kacey's hips for balance though I knew he didn't need it. Kacey growled again and spun towards Rick but Rick had already turned to point at me. "A hundred on who takes him down?"

I just grinned in response and took off towards the side of the house closest to me, leaving Rick to take the other side.

Once I rounded the house I didn't see any movement, it was silent as I moved along the back landing.

Suddenly, there was movement from the corner of my eye, and I spun towards it, my gun at the ready. It was Stine, trying to make a run for the back fence.

"Gotcha," I muttered under my breath, taking off after him.

Stine was fast, but I was faster. I could hear his ragged breathing as he stumbled through the overgrown grass, trying to outrun me. But I wasn't about to let him slip away again. I closed the distance between us quickly, and just as he was about to vault the fence, I tackled him from behind, slamming him into the ground. Stine let out a grunt as he hit the dirt, and I quickly restrained him, pinning him to the ground with my knee. Stine struggled beneath me, cursing and flailing, but I kept a firm grip on him, my gun pressed against the back of his head.

"Nice one," Rick said as he jogged up, a smug expression on his face. "Looks like I owe you a hundred bucks."

I just chuckled after yanking Stine off the ground. Rick did a thorough pat down, finding two guns before I handed him over to Kacey, who had followed Rick around the side of the house.

Kacey dragged Stine back around to the front of the house, opting to put the restrained man into the trunk of his vehicle for the return trip. I could understand his reasoning for not wanting to look at the traitor since I personally wanted to cause him pain also and wasn't sure how long I could have sat in the back seat with him without doing exactly that.

A tiny sense of accomplishment trickled into my mind. We were one step closer to rescuing Lexi, and every victory, no matter how small, was a step in the right direction.

But my relief was short-lived as my phone rang, and I saw Colt's name flash on the screen. I answered it quickly, my heart pounding in my chest.

"We didn't get Corletti," Colt said, his voice tense. "This location hasn't been used for weeks from the look of it."

I frowned at that. "So that means Corletti was in on Dominick's escape and wherever he is we might find Dominick and therefore Lexi?"

Colt let out a sigh. "That's what I'm thinking. We need to regroup and figure out our next move."

I nodded, even though he couldn't see me. "Got it. We managed to catch Stine, we are bringing him back to the warehouse."

"Good work," Colt said. "I'll meet you there as soon as I can. We need to interrogate him and see if he knows anything about Corletti's or Dominick's whereabouts."

"Understood," I replied, ending the call.

I turned to Kacey and Rick, who were both looking at me expectantly. "Corletti wasn't there," I said, relaying Colt's message. "But he must have been in on the escape."

Kacey nodded. "So where do we go from here?"

"We're bringing Stine back to the warehouse for interrogation," I said. "Maybe he knows something that can help us find them."

Kacey nodded again as we all got back into the car and started heading back, our thoughts loud around us.

Rick was the one to break the silence. "So, back to my question," he said leaning towards Kacey's seat, "have you ever been fucked by a criminal?"

I could see a touch of heat creep up the back of Kacey's neck from where I sat in the back seat as he shot Rick a glare.

Rick continued to push, ignoring Kacey's obvious annoyance. "I mean, you must have had some wild experiences with all the dangerous men you've been around," he said with a smirk. "Maybe I could show you what a real criminal can do."

Rick's tone was playful, but there was a hint of seduction in his voice that made me roll my eyes. Kacey's eyes flickered toward me for a moment, and I could tell he was debating whether to respond or not.

Finally, he let out a small laugh. "Sorry to disappoint you, Rick, but my love life doesn't involve criminals," he said, his tone light but firm.

Rick raised his eyebrows, a smirk playing on his lips. "Well, there's always a first time for everything," he said, winking at Kacey.

Kacey rolled his eyes and tried to ignore Rick's advances, focusing instead on the road. But Rick wasn't one to give up easily. He started to lean in closer, whispering in Kacey's ear, "Come on, Kace, you know you want to. Let me show you what it's like to be with a real bad boy."

I heard Kacey growl before he leaned over to turn the radio on and up in an attempt to drown Rick out. I laughed and let my head fall back against the seat as I closed my eyes and ignored everything else. Sleep and exhaustion instantly dragged me under.

Chapter 7

Gabe

55 HRS SINCE EXPLOSION

With most of the team out pursuing leads I was feeling useless. I wanted Lexi back so badly, but there was nothing I could contribute until they returned with their targets. I had taken the opportunity to try to get a few hours of sleep. I knew that being well-rested would help me stay focused and alert for whatever lay ahead. Fortunately, the warehouse had several rooms tucked away down a back corridor, including one specifically designed with bunks for this exact purpose.

I left the door cracked open in order to hear if I was needed but then the exhaustion I felt at barely sleeping for days dragged me under almost the moment I laid down.

When I awoke, it felt as though only moments had passed. Disorientation set in as my surroundings came into focus. In my haze, I reached out for Lexi to cuddle into, seeking her familiar warmth and comfort. Her absence hit me like a punch to the gut, and a sense of loss enveloped me. My heart felt like it was gripped in a vise, the realization that Lexi was still missing and the uncertainty of her fate weighed heavily on me.

I dragged myself out of the bed. I knew that I hadn't gotten nearly enough sleep, but with thoughts of Lexi swirling around my mind, I knew I wasn't going to be able to fall asleep again.

As my hand reached for the doorknob, ready to push it open, the sound of footsteps and voices reached my ears, causing me to pause. I peered through the narrow crack of the slightly open door and caught sight of Ashley walking down the corridor with Beckett trailing behind her.

"Please, Ash, we need to talk," Beckett pleaded with her in a hushed voice, his tone tinged with desperation.

But Ashley's response was immediate and firm. "No, Beck, I don't want to talk about it. Just go back to your computer."

Beckett's frustration was palpable as he grabbed her arm to stop her from walking away. I could see the anger flashing across his face, and for a moment, I contemplated stepping in to diffuse the situation.

But before I could do anything, Beckett had moved Ashley back against the wall of the corridor, holding her in place with both hands. "You know," he began to say but was quickly interrupted.

Beck released her as Nix appeared in the entryway to the hall, and I could see the frustration and anger on Beck's face. He growled before he spun towards the entrance once more, and started storming away. "Fix this," he growled with a wave of a hand in Ashley's direction before he disappeared.

Nix's attention was all on Ashley as he prowled over to where she was still standing against the wall. The tension in the air was palpable as they faced each other, their body language communicating volumes. Ashley looked hesitant and unsure, while Nix exuded confidence and a sense of authority.

"Surely you understand. We are growing tired of waiting," he growled at her, his voice laced with frustration and impatience.

"I just need time," I heard her whisper, her voice barely audible.

Nix's voice softened as he leaned in closer to her. "We have given you years, Mon Ange. Once we rescue Lexi, you're out of time," he said, his words almost a threat.

Ashley shook her head slightly, her expression pained. "But it's wrong. What we feel is wrong," she murmured.

Without warning, Nix reached up and wrapped a tattooed hand around her throat, stepping even closer to her, his other hand resting on the wall near her head. The sudden violence of his action made me gasp in shock, and I hesitated for a moment, unsure of what to do.

"You know what they say, it's better when it feels wrong," he breathed against her lips before kissing her with such passion that it made me feel guilty for watching their intimate moment.

Ashley let out a small moan as Nix continued to kiss her, his hand still wrapped tightly around her throat. But then, she tore her face away from Nix's and spoke sadly. "We can't do this, Mon Loup," she said, using the nickname she had for him. She pulled herself from his grasp and ducked under his arm, quickly exiting the corridor and disappearing from view.

Nix just watched her go with an exhausted sigh before he glanced back toward where I was hidden in the bunk room. "I know you're there."

After a few moments of hesitation, I decided to face him. Slowly, I stepped out of the bunk room and into the corridor. Nix was leaning against the wall, his arms crossed over his chest. He regarded me with a level gaze, and for a moment, I couldn't read his expression.

Finally, he spoke. "You shouldn't have been listening in on our conversation," he said sternly. "It's not your place to know about our personal lives."

"I'm sorry," I responded quickly, feeling guilty for overhearing their conversation. "I didn't mean to eavesdrop. I was just... worried."

Nix nodded, his demeanor softening slightly as he spoke. "I can understand your curiosity, but our relationship with Ash is complex, and we prefer to keep it private. We don't usually discuss it with outsiders," he explained.

"I completely understand and respect that," I assured him.

However, my next statement seemed to catch him off guard. "You do know that we're all in a relationship with Lexi, right? All of us," I said, emphasizing the last three words.

Nix raised an eyebrow in surprise. "I suspected that Colt had a relationship with her, but I had no idea about the rest of you," he said, mulling over the information. "Does Ashley know about this?" he inquired.

I shook my head. "No, unfortunately. Lexi cut off all communication with Ashley when she came to the safe house with us. We all grew close to Lexi, and then she was taken. Ashley and Lexi haven't spoken since before we met her," I explained.

Nix furrowed his brows at the new information. "Perhaps they should speak more when Lexi is back. However, our desire for Ashley wasn't her main concern. Despite the fact that she didn't come to live with us until she was a teenager, we are still her foster brothers," he said with a troubled expression.

I couldn't help but chuckle at his statement. "Yeah, I can't really help you with that one," I admitted, shrugging my shoulders.

He chuckled also and shook his head. "I was actually coming to get you. Corletti wasn't there but the others have Stine and are bringing him back here. We need to set up a room in preparation."

I nodded. "I think there is a cold room that we could use, the walls should be solid enough so no one can hear anything. We can put a chair in there to secure him while we try to get the information we need out of him."

Nix looked at me thoughtfully. "Good idea. And we'll need to make sure the chair is bolted to the floor so he can't tip it over or escape. I'm sure we have the supplies to accomplish that."

I could sense a darker energy in the air as we discussed the best way to extract information from Stine. It was clear that we were willing to go to any lengths to get the intel we needed. Nix's expression was steely and determined, his mind now focused on the task at hand.

I gestured for Nix to follow me as we made our way to the cold room. The atmosphere was tense as we worked to secure the chair to the floor.

As we finished our preparations, I could feel my heart racing with anticipation. Stine had the information that we needed, and we were not going to let him get away without giving it up. He was the closest we had come to finding Lexi since she was taken from us.

Nix stood back and inspected our work, making sure that everything was secure and that there was no chance of Stine escaping. He nodded his approval and we stepped out of the room, closing the heavy metal door behind us.

Now we just had to wait for the others to return with Stine.

Chapter 8

Alexis

58 HRS SINCE EXPLOSION

I must have passed out. Or fallen asleep. It was hard to tell which one with how disorientated my mind was becoming. My wrists were pulling painfully against the metal around them where they were held up against the wall, my head had fallen forward as much as it could and the pain in my neck as I lifted it in the darkness made me whimper.

I didn't know what time it was, but based on the previous visits I could assume that Enzo the asshole would let me out of the chains to sleep at some point.

Based on the pieces of information I had put together from the different visits, I could assume that the visits from Nick were sometime in the morning, while Enzo then let me down to sleep in the evening.

I took a deep breath, trying to focus on my surroundings. The room was pitch black, and I couldn't see anything. I could only hear my own breathing and the sound of my heart beating frantically in my chest. I tried to wiggle my fingers and toes to keep the blood flowing, but the chains held me in place.

Suddenly, I heard a faint noise coming from outside the door. My heart raced as I strained to listen more closely. Footsteps. It sounded like someone was approaching.

The light coming back on almost blinded me and made stars appear in my vision.

It was the same two women as last time, once again with medical supplies and food. I tried to keep my breathing steady as they moved around the room, checking my wounds and giving me water and food.

After seeing the fresh bruises and cuts on the one that Enzo had manhandled I knew I couldn't inflict more of that suffering on either of them, I had to remain silent for their sakes. As the women finished tending to my wounds, they gave me a sad smile before leaving the room, passing a smirking Enzo in the doorway.

I balled my hands into tight fists as Enzo strutted into the room, a malevolent smirk on his face. The way his eyes gleamed with sadistic glee made me shudder. I knew I was in for another round of psychological torture.

His fingers traced my cheek, and I flinched at the cold, rough sensation. The chains kept me anchored in place, unable to move away from his touch. He reveled in my discomfort, delighting in the control he held over me.

And then he uttered the words that made my blood run cold. "You want to know what sound lives rent-free in my head?" His voice was low and menacing, like a predator toy-ing with its prey. "The sound of your screams as that one guy flew through the air and fell all the way to the ground floor dead."

The memory of that horrific moment flooded my mind, and I felt a sob clawing its way up my throat. I bit my lip, trying to hold it in, but the pain was too much.

Enzo leaned in closer, his hot breath tickling my ear. "I wonder how long it'll take Dominick to break you," he whispered, his tone dripping with malice. "Maybe once he has, he'll let me have a taste of you."

I felt a tear escape my eye and roll down my cheek, and before I could even react, Enzo licked it off my face, causing my stomach to churn with disgust. The mere thought of what he might do to me made me want to retch.

I knew that Enzo was trying to break me down, to make me feel weak and helpless. But I refused to give him the satisfaction. I held on to my inner strength and refused to let him break me.

In a move he didn't see coming I slammed my head against his as best I could since he was so close. Pain exploded inside my head but I still heard the satisfying crunch as his nose broke.

Enzo stumbled back, clutching his nose and cursing loudly. I could feel blood trickling down my face, but the pain was worth it to see the look of shock and anger on his face.

For a moment, there was silence in the room as Enzo and I glared at each other. I could see the fury in his eyes, and I knew that I had just made things so much worse for myself. But I refused to back down. I refused to let Enzo or Dominick or anyone else control me. I would fight back, no matter what the cost.

With a deep breath, I braced myself for whatever was to come. I had no idea what Enzo or Dominick had planned for me next, but I was determined to face it head-on.

Enzo recovered quickly and lunged at me, his rage consumed him as he seized me by the throat, his fingers squeezing with a crushing force that made me feel like my windpipe was collapsing. I gasped for breath, but he didn't let up. His other hand pressed down hard on the wounds that covered my ribs, each touch causing searing pain to shoot through my body. I tried to wiggle free, but he held me in place with a grip of iron.

"You stupid bitch," he hissed, spittle flying from his lips. "You're lucky that Nick still wants you alive, or I'd kill you right here and now. But mark my words, once he's done with you, I'll make you pay for what you've done. You'll regret the day you crossed us."

Enzo's words made my blood run cold. The thought of what he was capable of filled me with dread. He seemed to take pleasure in the pain of others, relishing in the agony of those he had tortured. The images that his words conjured up made bile rise in my throat, and I felt a wave of nausea wash over me.

"I'm going to make you scream," he continued, his grip on my throat tightening even more. "I'm going to cut you and fuck you until you're nothing but a whimpering, broken mess. And then, when I'm done with you, I'll make sure you beg for death."

I glared at him, my eyes blazing with defiance, determined not to let him break me. But deep down, I knew that he was capable of anything, and I feared what would happen if he ever got his hands on me again.

As Enzo tightened his grip on my throat, I gasped for air, but refused to give him the satisfaction of begging for mercy. Instead, I used all my strength to push against him, trying to break free from his hold.

But Enzo was too strong, too relentless. He laughed as I struggled, his grip tightening even more. I felt my vision start to fade as I gasped for air, my body starting to go limp.

Just as I thought I was about to lose consciousness he released his hold on me and left the room, turning off the lights the moment the door closed.

He hadn't let me down from the chains, and I doubted that he would return to do that after what I had just done. It meant I was going to be spending a long stretch of time in this same position chained upright to the wall.

My neck and ribs throbbed with pain, and my head was pounding from the lack of oxygen. But I refused to give up. I refused to let anyone break me. I had survived dying at Dominick's hands once already and I had seen them kill the men that were becoming my world. There was nothing more they could do to me.

I took a deep breath and tried to steady myself. The darkness was suffocating, but I knew I had to keep my wits about me. I had to keep my mind sharp and alert, even in the face of this torment. I knew I couldn't let Enzo or Dominick win. They wanted me to feel weak, to feel helpless, but I refused to give them that satisfaction.

I closed my eyes and focused on my breathing, trying to block out the pain and the fear. I had to stay strong, no matter what.

But for now, all I could do was endure. Endure the pain, the fear, the uncertainty. I had no idea what was going to happen next, but I knew that I had to be ready for anything.

I hung there in the darkness, listening to the sound of my own breathing and the thumping of my heart. I tried to block out the memories of the past, the guilt, the regret, the pain. Instead, I focused on the present moment, on the task at hand: surviving.

I don't know how long I hung there, chained to the wall in the darkness.

Chapter 9

Colt

59 HRS SINCE EXPLOSION

You might think you can prepare yourself mentally to torture someone. You can't.

I was letting Nix's team take the lead on extracting the information we wanted from Stine. It wasn't something that was unfamiliar to them after all. I had never seen it personally but I knew they worked like a well oiled torture machine.

After helping Kacey secure Stine in the chair in the cold room that Gabe and Nix prepared, we stepped back to lean against the wall as the others also entered the room. As much as I wasn't going to be participating, I needed to be here to witness it. I needed him to tell us where Dominick had taken Lexi.

As the door closed behind us, I braced myself for what was to come. The room was cold, and the sound of the metal chair scraping against the concrete floor echoed loudly in the enclosed space. Stine looked up at us with a mixture of fear and defiance in his eyes, knowing full well what was about to happen.

"Torture me all you like, I'm not telling you shit," he spat out at us.

Nix scoffed at him. "We'll see about that."

Nix's team worked with ruthless efficiency, their movements precise and calculated as they began their work. The sounds that echoed around the room were brutal and guttural as Rick started to land blow after blow across various parts of Stine's body, dragging pain filled grunts from Stine that bounced off the walls.

As much as I wanted to look away, I couldn't. I needed to see this through, to know that we were getting the information we needed to save Lexi.

The minutes stretched on like hours and before long Beck had replaced Rick and was starting to break each bone in Stine's body, beginning with his fingers; the sound of Stine's cries filled the air.

But Stine refused to give in. He was, after all, a fully trained ex-US Marshal. And also a stubborn asshole.

Despite the pain and torment that Nix's team inflicted upon him, Stine remained tight-lipped. His body was battered and bruised, his face contorted in agony, but he refused to break. It was both admirable and infuriating.

As the hours ticked by, the frustration in the room grew palpable.

And all the while, I couldn't help but think about Lexi. What was happening to her right now? Was she even still alive?

Nix crouched down in front of Stine. "You know what comes next right?" he asked before holding up a sharp knife for Stine to see. "You could make this easy on yourself and tell us what we want to know."

Stine groaned as he adjusted in his seat. "You're just going to kill me anyway so have at it."

Nix chucked in response. "Yes, that is probably true, but it's completely up to you on how fast we get to that point and how much more pain we inflict on you in the meantime."

Stine just glared at him before he continued, "You see, if you tell us what we need to know then my friend here can shoot you nice and quick."

Rick leveled the barrel of a gun against his temple and just flicked his glare in Stine's direction before looking back to Nix, awaiting his signal.

"Or, I can take this knife and start carving you up piece by piece until you finally give us what we want," Nix finished his sentence, his voice low and menacing.

Stine sneered at him. "You think that scares me? You think I got into bed with criminals like them without knowing I could expect worse than this? You have a long way to go to scare me, kid."

Nix's chuckle is low and menacing. "Well, it's a good thing we are only just getting started then right?"

He nodded to Beck who grabbed hold of one of Stine's hands, uncurling the fist he was holding it in and stretching it out against the arm of the chair while Nix sharpened the knife ominously.

He held the knife up to the light as though he was inspecting it. "You know I read this book once, where the main character used to slice her victims where their fingers bent so that it was both extra painful and they could never bend them the same again."

He moved the knife to rest the sharp edge against the bend of Stine's index finger before he paused thoughtfully. "But then, it's not like you will be using your fingers again anyway so I guess I don't have to be quite as delicate."

With that, he cut deeply and slowly into the flesh of Stine's finger. Stine's screams echoed around the room in increasing intensity as Nix made his way slowly through each of Stine's fingers until they were all a bleeding mess of flesh and bone. His blood was slowly dripping down onto the concrete floor beneath the chair.

But still, he didn't break.

The next hour was a symphony of Stine's screams as Nix slowly and methodically cut into the most sensitive parts of his body.

But finally, after what felt like an eternity, Stine broke. He begged for mercy, spilling everything he knew. Which wasn't much at all.

He didn't know where Dominick was holding Lexi. The only person he dealt with was Enzo Corletti. Who wasn't anywhere to be found.

But after some further persuasion, he was able to recite the number he was made to memorize if he needed to call him. Rome took the number down before disappearing out the door with Beckett following after him. I'm sure both were headed back to their computers to search for Enzo's location obsessively.

Nix leaned in closer to Stine, the knife still held loosely in his hand. "See, that wasn't so hard now, was it?" he said with a smirk.

Stine gasped for air, his body shaking with pain and exhaustion. "Please...just let me go, I won't tell them you're looking, I'll hide out until you take care of them," he pleaded weakly. He had truly been broken and was now a weak sniveling mess.

Nix shook his head. "I'm afraid it's too late for that," he replied coldly.

Stine's eyes widened in fear as he realized what Nix was implying. "No, please..." he begged, but it was too late.

Nix nodded to Rick, who raised his gun and fired a single shot, ending Stine's life instantly.

The room fell silent, except for the sound of the gun echoing off the walls.

Nix glanced over his shoulder at me. "We will clean this up, go get some rest while Beck and Rome try to find Enzo."

I could see the weariness weighing down on him but before I could say anything Ash stepped forward and laid a hand on the back of his shoulder. It startled me, having completely forgotten that she was even in the room.

"I'll clean it up. You go rest too," she said softly before she started to move around the room, Nix just stared at her for a moment before he sighed and walked out the door.

Chapter 10

Alexis

71 HRS SINCE EXPLOSION

Once again I woke to Nick sitting casually in a chair facing me playing with a knife while I hung limply from the chains on the wall. I was thankful that I had barely drunk anything since being there apart from a few sips of water because they obviously had no consideration for their torture victims needing to use the toilet.

Nick noticed me awake and grinned, "Good morning, Fiore Mio. Did you have a nice nap?"

I glared at him, the hatred in my eyes stronger than ever before. "You're a sick bastard."

Nick stood up from his chair and approached me. He pressed the tip of the knife against my cheek, tracing a line down my jawline. "You know, you're quite beautiful when you're asleep," he said, his voice low and almost seductive.

I flinched away from him as much as possible, but the chains limited my movement. "Go to hell," I spat at him.

He chucked in response. "Oh, you're already there, darling. But back to watching you sleep, you know the best part?"

I remained silent, not wanting to give him the satisfaction of a response.

Nick leaned in closer to me, his breath hot on my face. "The best part is the dreams you have," he whispered. "I was watching you for a while, and your dreams are quite entertaining. Especially when you cried out for... Colt was it? How you begged him not to die. How you blame yourself for his death."

I closed my eyes tightly, trying to block out his words and the memories of my nightmares.

I felt him move away from me again and opened my eyes to see the satisfaction on his face at my only show of weakness.

He smirked. "What happened to Colt, Fiore Mio?"

My eyes blazed as I glared at him. "Your lapdog and his men killed him and his team."

Nick chuckled, twirling the knife in his hand. "Ah yes, I re-member Enzo telling me now. You were quite the firecracker that day from what I heard." He leaned in close to me again. "But why blame yourself for his death? It's not like you could have stopped it."

I gritted my teeth, refusing to answer him.

He laughed and stepped back. "Speaking of my lapdog as you called him, I saw your little handiwork on his face. You know I'm proud of you that you managed to do that while still chained to a wall."

I grinned at him savagely. "Lose the knife and come over here and I'll make you proud again."

Nick chuckled, but his eyes darkened with a dangerous glint. "Feisty as ever, I see. But let's not get ahead of ourselves, my dear. We have so much more to explore before we get to the fun part."

I narrowed my eyes at him, trying to hide the fear that was creeping up inside me. "What more could you possibly want from me?"

Nick leaned in close to me again, the knife still twirling in his hand. "Oh, so much, my dear. You see, I want to break you. I want to see the fire in your eyes turn to fear and desperation. I want to hear you beg for mercy and plead for your life." He traced the tip of the knife along my collarbone, leaving a trail of cold metal against my skin.

I shuddered at his words and the sensation of the knife on my skin. "You won't break me," I said through gritted teeth, trying to sound confident despite the fear that was beginning to take hold.

Nick chuckled, his breath hot on my neck. "Oh, I will, Fiore Mio. I will break you."

I felt a surge of anger and defiance inside me, despite the fear that was still creeping up. I wouldn't let him break me. I wouldn't give him the satisfaction. I took a deep breath and met his gaze head-on.

"You can try all you want, Nick," I said firmly. "But I won't break. I won't give in to your sick, twisted games."

Nick's grin widened, and I could see the madness in his eyes. "We'll see about that, Fiore Mio. We'll see."

I stiffened at his words, knowing what was coming next. Nick stepped back from me, twirling the knife in his hand once again, and I braced myself for what was to come.

There was no distraction and I felt the moment the blade entered the skin on my ribs and slid across that side of my body. The pain was like a wildfire that swept through me and I couldn't hold back the whimper that broke free from behind my clenched jaw.

I squeezed my eyes tightly to try to shut out my reality as Nick chuckled in my ear, enjoying the sound of my pain.

The pain started to fade away and I opened my eyes again and panted out a breath, just as Nick pushed his blade into the flesh on the other side and slowly dragged it across my ribs.

I couldn't stop the scream this time and I heard Nick moan at hearing the sound ripped from me. "You didn't think that what you did to Enzo would go unpunished right?" he breathed into my ear as I whimpered in pain.

He dropped the knife onto the ground with a sharp clatter before using the fingers of both hands to push savagely at the cuts he made in my skin. Pain tore through me again, drawing another involuntary scream from my lips.

He moaned again, "Your screams are like listening to porn. I've lost count of the number of times I came to the memories of your screams in that alleyway." He pressed his erection against me as he twisted his fingers in my wounds.

Nausea rushed through me and tears streamed down my face as I tried to catch my breath, my body trembling.

I felt sick to my stomach as I tried to hold back the bile rising in my throat. Nick leaned in close to me, his hot breath on my ear, and whispered, "You belong to me now. Remember that."

I wanted to fight back, to tell him that I wouldn't be his plaything, but the pain was too much, and I could barely think straight. I tried to focus on my breathing, to push the pain aside and find some strength, but it was all too overwhelming.

Nick's hand moved down to my thigh, gripping it tightly as he leaned in to kiss me. I turned my head away, but he grabbed my chin and forced me to face him. His lips crashed onto mine, and I could taste the blood in my mouth.

I held in the sobs that threatened to spill out as he bit at my lip before stepping away from me. The color of my blood was smeared across his mouth once again as he grinned maniacally before retrieving the knife and leaving me in the dark again.

I felt violated, helpless, and alone. The pain was unbearable, and I knew that I was not going to be able to get out of this without help. But who would come to my rescue?

Chapter 11

Rome

72 HRS SINCE EXPLOSION

I felt like my eyes were burning. I had been staring at my computer almost constantly for three days. When Stine gave us the number we thought we would be able to easily locate Enzo and therefore Dominick. What we hadn't counted on was the phone being off and not transmitting any tracking details to find its history. We were still digging into all avenues to try to get a location but it's as though it were a basic burner specifically made to stay off the radar.

Whilst the big screen showed the constant search for the phone signal Beck and I had gone back to scouring the internet for anything on Dominick and his minions.

We hit dead ends everywhere we turned. It was as though Dominick didn't exist, and his minions were just a figment of our imagination. We had tried every search engine and every database we could think of, but nothing came up. It was frustrating, to say the least.

As we sat in silence, scrolling through pages of useless information, I couldn't help but feel defeated. It seemed like the more we searched, the less progress we made. It was as though we were spinning our wheels, going nowhere fast.

As I rubbed my tired eyes, I couldn't help but feel frustrated with the lack of progress we were making. Dominick was a slippery target, and it seemed like every lead we pursued ended up being a dead end. I glanced over at Beck, who was hunched over his computer with a look of intense concentration on his face.

"Anything new?" I asked him, hoping for a glimmer of hope in our search.

Beck shook his head, his eyes still fixed on his screen. "No, nothing yet. I'm starting to think that Dominick has scrubbed the internet clean of any mention of himself or his organization."

I groaned in frustration. "This is ridiculous. How are we supposed to find him if he doesn't want to be found?"

"We just have to keep digging," Beck replied, sounding more determined than ever. "There has to be something out there that we can use to track him down. We just have to find it."

I nodded in agreement, feeling a renewed sense of determination. We had come too far to give up now.

With that in mind, I turned my attention back to my computer to resume my search but a sharp noise startled me and made my attention focus instead on the big screen on the wall. That now had a small red dot blinking in the middle of a map.

"Fuck. Record that before it disappears! It's Enzo!" I shouted.

Beck sprang into action, taking a screenshot and recording the location details seconds before the red dot disappeared once again into oblivion like it was never there to begin with and the screen went back to the view of the whole country as it resumed its search again.

"Bring the location back up." I demanded, I was probably being harsher than I should have with a friend but finding this breadcrumb was everything to me.

Beck brought the map of the location back up onto the screen.

I squinted at what I was seeing, not recognizing anything around the location. "Where the hell is that?"

Beck pulled the map further out and consulted the computer. "About six hours from here."

My heart sank at the thought of another long journey, but I knew we had to act fast. We couldn't afford to waste any time.

"I'll go let the others know. Can you start getting the vehicles ready?" I asked as I made my way towards the door to the room, heading towards where the others were getting some rest.

After Beck agreed I moved down the back corridor and into the bunk room. Colt was already awake staring into the distance as I made my way to him. His attention snapped to me when I approached.

"We have a location." I said without preamble and he was out of bed in an instant.

Colt nodded, looking serious. "Let's go then. We don't have any time to waste. Where is he?"

I explained the location to him and he nodded in understanding. "I'll go round up the others and get everyone ready. How soon can we leave?"

"Beck is getting the vehicles ready now. We need to move fast," I added, "We don't know how long Enzo will stay in one place."

Within minutes, we were all packed up and ready to go. Beck had the vehicles prepped and waiting for us.

After briefing everyone on the location we were headed, Nix stressed to everyone that as much as we wanted to go in guns blazing we needed to assess the situation and hold off to enter under the cover of nightfall so they didn't run or potentially kill Lexi at the first sign of a rescue.

We piled into the two SUVs and started the six-hour journey to the location we had managed to find. The atmosphere in the car was tense, and everyone was silent, lost in their thoughts.

I rested my head against the cold glass of the window and closed my eyes, the last three days finally catching up to me now that I wasn't deep in search mode. Exhaustion pulled me into a restless uncomfortable sleep.

The drive felt never-ending, and I felt like I had been sleeping for hours when I was jolted awake by the sound of gravel crunching under the tires. I rubbed my eyes and looked out the window to see that we had finally arrived at our destination.

The area was remote and desolate, and I couldn't see any signs of life. We parked the cars at a safe distance and huddled together to come up with a plan of action.

After a quick discussion, we split up into two groups. Nix, Colt, Beck, and Hunt would scout out the area and assess the situation, while the rest of us would stay back and keep watch in case anything went wrong.

As I sat in the car with my eyes fixed on the surrounding area, I couldn't help but feel nervous. We had come so far, and the thought of something going wrong was almost too much to bear.

Minutes turned into hours, and the sun slowly started to dip below the horizon. The tension in the air was palpable as we waited for the others to return. Every minute that passed felt like an eternity, and my mind was racing with all the worst-case scenarios.

Finally, I saw them making their way back under the limited cover of the trees and my heart leaped with hope while we rushed over for the report.

Nix spoke first, his voice steady and controlled. "We've found the location of the house. It's heavily guarded, but we think we can take them by surprise if we move in under the cover of darkness."

I took a deep breath, feeling the weight of the situation settling heavily on my shoulders. "Okay, let's do this. We're not leaving without Lexi."

With a renewed sense of determination, we set about finalizing our plan and getting into position.

We were trying to utilize the skills of each of our teams as best we could. Given the extra security that surrounded the location, we armed our sharpshooters in the teams with hi-powered rifles and pointed them to higher ground for better vantage points. We knew that the moment the first guard spotted us, our approach would basically be announced.

The reconnaissance had determined that a majority of their force was centered outside of the building to stop anything before it made it inside to where Dominick's inner circle was.

While we waited for the recon team to do their thing, Gabe and Rick put their crazy minds together to create some variation of a grenade crossed with a Molotov cocktail that as part of its explosion would launch flaming shrapnel in every direction. But not to take any chances they were also loaded down with flash grenades and smoke bombs along with normal explosives and their own firearms.

The rest of us were also loaded with firearms and explosives.

As we all took position around the property I played the plan back over in my head. We would be hitting from all sides at the same time. We didn't want Dominick or Enzo escaping but we also didn't want to allow enough time for them to hurt Lexi because we were there.

We took a moment to all check in from our positions, Ash being the last with, "Eagle eye checking in. It's a beautiful night for a rescue don't you think?"

I took a moment to breathe in deeply and center myself. This was it, the moment we had been working towards for days. It was time to bring Lexi home.

Chapter 12

Alexis

82 HRS SINCE EXPLOSION

When Dominick stabbed me two years ago, it hadn't been quick but it also hadn't been drawn out like he was doing now. He was taking a sick perverted pleasure from drawing out my torture.

I had thankfully not passed out again after his last visit but on the down side that meant the pain filled time stretched out like an eternity.

There was a shiver that had started not long before from the cold and I was having to keep moving and curling my fingers and toes to keep the blood flow to them or they started to go numb. The pain in my wrists from the metal cuffs that chained me to the wall was almost as painful as the cuts to the skin on my ribs. The flesh had been torn from constantly trying to pull free and I could tell that there was blood from the cuts on my wrists because as it dried it was pulling at the skin and hairs on my arms.

I could only imagine what a gruesome sight I was considering the darkness that surrounded me. I knew that most of me was probably covered in dirt and blood.

I tried to push the pain aside and focus on the sounds outside. I heard footsteps and voices, but they were distant and muffled. It could be anyone, so I tried not to get my hopes up that someone would at least let me down from the chains, even for a few hours.

But then I heard a sound that made my heart leap with hope. It was the sound of gunfire, followed by explosions. It was chaos outside, and for a moment, I allowed myself to believe that it was my rescuers.

The sound of the door crashing open brought me back to reality. I squinted against the sudden brightness as two people rushed into the room. I couldn't see their faces from the light behind them, but I could tell they were armed and dangerous.

"Holy fuck." A voice breathed out and I knew then that I must be hallucinating. The voice was so familiar to me, but it couldn't be him, I had watched him die. The pain and darkness must have finally tipped me into madness.

"Find the fucking light switch, now." The voice snapped at his partner as he slowly and tentatively stepped toward me.

Suddenly the overhead light came on, nearly blinding me completely. And standing before me was my hallucination. My Colt.

I couldn't stop the whimper as I squeezed my eyes shut against the pain of this hallucination. "You aren't real. I saw you die." I whispered with a slight shake of my head.

I felt a tentative touch against my cheek, the fingers so soft, like they were afraid to touch me in case they hurt me.

"Princess. It is me. Look at me, show me those pretty eyes," he whispered back to me.

I blinked open my eyes again and looked into his familiar green eyes and a sob escaped me. I never thought I would ever see those eyes look at me again.

"That's it, princess. We're here, you're safe now." He rested his forehead softly against mine and I felt tears on my face. I hadn't even realized I started to cry but as he pulled back I saw I wasn't the only one.

I didn't recognize the man with him but he had somehow found keys to the chains attached to my arms. When he released me I instantly dropped towards the floor, my legs not having been used for so long meant they weren't going to hold me up.

Colt was quick and caught me in his arms, gently wrapping an arm under my malfunctioning legs and lifting me up to hold me close to his chest. He was trying to be as gentle as possible but it still hurt like a bitch, drawing another whimper from me.

"Are we good?" The question came from the other man.

"Give me a minute." Colt grunted as he held me close and simply stood there for a moment.

I could feel Colt's heart beating against my cheek as he held me, and I couldn't believe he was actually there. After everything that had happened, I never thought I would see him again.

I could hear the chaos and commotion outside, the sounds of gunfire and explosions still ringing in my ears. But none of it mattered as long as I was safe in Colt's arms. I couldn't believe he was real, that he was there to rescue me. I had thought he was dead, that I had lost him forever.

I buried my face into his chest and breathed in his familiar scent, trying to ground myself in the reality that he really was there and alive.

"Thank you," I whispered, tears still streaming down my face. "Thank you for coming for me."

"Always, princess," he murmured back, pressing a gentle kiss to my head. "I'll always come for you."

The other man cleared his throat, interrupting our moment. "We need to go. There could still be danger here."

Colt nodded and started to carry me towards the door, the other man following closely behind.

He carried me out of the room, and I clung to him tightly, not wanting to let go. I didn't care if this was a hallucination, it felt so real and I was going to hold on to it as long as I could.

We made our way through a maze of corridors, and I heard more gunfire and explosions in the distance. It seemed like a full-blown battle was happening outside, and I wondered what was going on.

Suddenly a shout close by drew our attention and then we heard a woman scream. I heard feet pounding against the ground heading towards us and Colt's partner dropped into a more braced stance with his gun aimed in the direction the sound was approaching from.

Enzo rounded the corner at a run. The moment he spotted us he tried to stop his momentum and his feet slid out from beneath him as he tried to change direction again. But then I saw another magical sight round the corner behind him. Rome came around the corner, gun raised and aimed at him.

Enzo's hands slowly raised into the air as he sneered at us. "You're going to regret this."

Colt's partner scoffed, "No we really won't." He continued holding his gun at Enzo as Rome secured restraints around Enzo's wrists and then bent his arms to force him to stand again.

It was the first time I had seen him since the headbutt that I had inflicted and it made me feel good to see the intense bruising and bandages that covered his nose and the blackened skin around his eyes.

Colt tilted his head as he looked Enzo over. "Your handiwork, princess?" he asked and I gave a small nod in response before he continued, "Good work, princess."

Rome's head snapped toward us and he shoved Enzo in the direction of the other man before moving quickly to stand in front of me. His eyes quickly took me in before he gently brushed some dirty strands of hair from my face, leaning in to rest his forehead against mine.

"Baby girl," he said softly before placing a feather light kiss on my temple.

The noise downstairs had died down now, the gunfire and explosions reduced to only the occasional pop.

I almost cried again when Gabe rounded the corner behind Rome.

His eyes widened and he was next to us in seconds. "Lexi," he breathed, his voice rough with emotion. He cradled my face ever so gently before he too placed a soft kiss against my cheek.

He looked at Colt before reporting, "Nothing else back there but two abused women. No Dominick."

Enzo laughed. "You stupid fucks, did you really think he would be here? He's only ever here long enough to torture that bitch and then he leaves."

Gabe moved over to him and landed a punch directly to his mouth.

Enzo stumbled and the other man with them had to grab him to prevent him from falling. "Shut the fuck up," Gabe snarled. "You don't get to talk about her like that."

Colt's partner grabbed Enzo's hair, pulling his head back. "Where is he?" He demanded.

Enzo just laughed again, blood trickling from his mouth. "Like I'm going to tell you."

Colt sighed, shaking his head. "Get him out of here. We'll interrogate him later."

The man led Enzo away, his laughter echoing down the hallway. Colt looked at me, concern etched on his face. "Are you okay?" he asked.

I nodded, feeling numb. "I just want to get out of here."

Colt nodded in agreement. Rome led the way out of the house with his gun taking out any straggling minions that crossed our path on the way while Gabe protected us from behind. I rested my head back against Colt and the moment we walked out into the night I took a deep breath of fresh air. I never thought I would get to do that again.

Colt's arms tightened around me as we walked outside. The adrenaline that had kept me going throughout the entire ordeal started to wear off and I felt a wave of exhaustion wash over me.

Chapter 13

Alexis

I must have passed out at some point because the next thing I knew, I was lying in a bed, wrapped in blankets.

I tried to move, but my body refused to cooperate. I was too weak and too sore to do anything. I could feel the bandages on my ribs, and I knew that I was going to be in pain for a while.

Looking around the room I had no idea where I was, but since I could remember being rescued, I figured I was safe somewhere. The room was small, and the bed was reasonably small, but considering my recent experience sleeping on a cold concrete floor and then chained to a wall, there was never going to be any complaint from me. There were two doorways, one that I could see led to a bathroom while the other that was currently closed must have led out of the room.

Dragging myself from the bed, I pushed past the pain and managed to use the toilet. I flat out refused to look at myself in the mirror, already knowing how much of a mess would reflect back at me, but I did note that someone had taken the time to clean me as best they could without completely disrespecting my dignity. I made my way back to the bed and laid back down, feeling the exhaustion and pain starting to catch up to me.

I must have dozed off again because the next thing I knew, Colt was sitting next to me, holding my hand. He looked exhausted, and there were bags under his eyes. But he was alive, and that was all that mattered.

"Hey, princess," he whispered, giving my hand a gentle squeeze. "How are you feeling?"

I tried to speak, but my throat was dry and scratchy. I managed a weak croak, "Better."

Colt smiled softly and reached for a glass of water on the bedside table, helping me take a sip. The cool liquid felt refreshing and soothing against my parched throat.

"We had a doc check you over and stitch up your cuts. He gave you some pain meds. You're going to be just fine physically. He suggested a checkup in a week or two," he mumbled as though he needed to get it out before he forgot.

I looked at him as he returned the glass, taking in all the features I never thought I would see again. "I thought I'd lost you. I thought you were dead."

A sob escaped me and before I knew it I couldn't stop, and my whole body was shaking as tears slid down my face. Colt was quick to cradle my face in his hand.

"Hey, It's okay, I'm here," Colt whispered, his voice filled with tenderness. "You're safe now."

He slowly and gently slid into the bed beside me, gathering my shaking body against him and stroking a hand gently through my hair.

I clung to him, feeling grateful for his comforting presence. It was all so overwhelming, and I didn't know how to process everything that had happened.

Colt held me until my sobs subsided, and I slowly regained my composure. He wiped away my tears with his thumb.

"What about Hunt?" I whispered after a moment, I had already seen that Rome and Gabe were ok but I had yet to see my sunshine.

Colt just pointed behind me and helped gently move me until I could see Hunt asleep in an armchair on the other side of the bed.

"I only just managed to get Rome and Gabe to go shower and rest since they had seen you awake, but he wouldn't leave until he saw you were okay for himself," he said.

I felt a rush of emotion seeing Hunt there, still by my side. I wanted to reach out and touch him, to feel his warmth and know that he was real.

"Thank you," I said softly to Colt, feeling a deep sense of gratitude toward him for everything he had done.

He gave me a small smile, "Anything for you, princess."

I felt a sense of peace wash over me, knowing that I was surrounded by people who cared for me. I closed my eyes, feeling exhaustion pulling me under again. But this time, I felt safe and secure, knowing that I was not alone.

I woke sometime later to the startling blue eyes of Hunt.

A small smile flicked across his lips at seeing me awake. "Hey, sweetheart," he said softly.

I could feel Colt still wrapped around me but judging from the steady slow beat of his heart and his soft breaths he had fallen deeply asleep.

"Hey." I responded quietly.

Hunt reached out to brush a strand of hair away from my face, his touch gentle and comforting. "How are you feeling?" he asked, concern etched on his face.

"I'm sore, but I'll be okay," I replied, my voice still weak.

He nodded, his gaze never leaving my face. "I'm sorry, sweetheart. I should have protected you better."

I shook my head, feeling tears welling up in my eyes again. "It's not your fault. You did everything you could to keep me safe."

Hunt leaned in and kissed me softly on the forehead, his lips warm against my skin. "I'm just glad you're okay."

"And are you okay?" I asked. "Last thing I saw that day was the house blowing up. I thought I had lost you all."

He nodded slightly. "It was close, but Gabe saw the explosives and we managed to keep everyone alive."

I hesitated for a moment before I asked the question I had tried not to think about since it happened. "Sam?"

"She's ok, and she has Nathan back," he responded.

A sense of relief flooded me, even though she had betrayed us it wasn't a choice she willingly made. I was glad to hear both she and Nathan were okay.

Colt moved slightly behind me, snuggling closer to my body and I froze, hoping I hadn't woken him by talking to Hunt.

Hunt chuckled softly. "I doubt he will be waking anytime soon, so long as you're in his arms again. He hasn't slept properly since you were taken." A sadness entered his face as he continued, "None of us have."

I felt a pang of guilt, knowing that my kidnapping had affected everyone so deeply. "I'm sorry," I said softly, feeling tears prick at my eyes again. "I didn't mean to cause so much trouble."

Hunt immediately shook his head, reaching out to grip my hand, his eyes intense as he looked at me. "You didn't cause any trouble, sweetheart. It was those bastards who took you. We're just glad to have you back."

We were silent for a while, just holding each other's hands and enjoying the peace and quiet. The events of the past few days left us all emotionally drained, and we needed time to process everything that happened.

After a while, Hunt leaned in and gave me a gentle kiss on the lips. "Get some rest, sweetheart. We'll be here when you wake up."

I closed my eyes, feeling the exhaustion take over once again. I felt at peace, knowing that I was safe and surrounded by people who cared for me. And as I drifted off to sleep, I knew that I found my home in their arms.

When I blinked my eyes open again it wasn't Hunt that sat in front of me, but someone I hadn't thought I would see again until Dominick was gone. Ashley sat facing me with her chin resting on her hands and a cheeky grin on her face. My eyes went wide at the sight of her and my mouth dropped open in shock.

"Luuucy, you have some splainin to do," she said in a sing-song voice. She leaned forward and said in a conspiratorial voice, "So how did you end up with my brother?"

Confusion filled me. "I'm sorry, what?" I stammered. Was I hallucinating again? Oh, that's right, I wasn't hallucinating before.

She giggled and flicked her eyes behind me where I still felt Colt curled around me.

"Brother?" I asked.

She nodded, still grinning at me like a loon. "Yep, small world right?!"

I was so lost and confused.

"Stop teasing, Ash." Colt grunted from behind me, finally awake. He softly kissed my shoulder before untangling himself from my body and sliding out of the bed.

Ash quickly covers her eyes before crying out, "Oh my god, are you naked? I don't want to see my brother's naked ass."

I laughed while Colt threw a pillow at Ash's face. She grinned and just focused on me. "It's good to hear you laugh. You scared the shit out of me."

I frowned again. "I'm sorry babe, I didn't mean to worry you by disappearing but I had no choice."

She just nodded as though that was a given. "Don't be sorry babe. Colt explained it all to me. I'm just glad you're okay."

Colt leaned down again and brushed a kiss against my forehead before standing and pointing a finger at Ash. "Exactly, so you can let her rest and sleep a little longer. You can catch up tomorrow before we move."

I looked at him quickly in surprise. "We are moving again?" I asked.

He focused back on me. "Yeah princess, so get some more rest for me okay."

With that, he headed toward the door, opening it and motioning for her to leave the room. She threw me a cheeky wink on her way out.

Colt hesitated for a moment, looking toward the window before he reached over to turn on the light. My heart skipped a beat at the gesture knowing that he was doing it for me to feel okay.

"Don't," I said to him, shaking my head.

He tilted his head and looked back at me curiously. "You don't want the light on?" he asked.

I closed my eyes for a moment before looking back at him, trying to push the words out. "While I was there, in that room, nothing happened to me while the lights were off. It was when the lights were on that I learned to become afraid of. They always made sure the lights were on when they hurt me."

Anger flashed over his face before he shut it down. Nodding, he turned the light back off for me. "Get some sleep, princess," he said softly before gently closing the door behind him.

I lay there for a moment, trying to process everything that just happened. Colt was Ash's brother? We were all together in another safe house? And we were moving again?

I sighed and closed my eyes, trying to push away the thoughts and focus on getting some more rest. My body felt heavy and lethargic, and I knew I needed more sleep if I was going to be able to face whatever challenges lay ahead.

Chapter 14

Colt

I waited for Ash to walk down the hallway towards the small living room in the apartment we were currently camped out in. It was a Black Wolf property so I didn't have any concern for our safety, but the tension of so many people in such a small space, especially Ash and the guys, I knew we couldn't stay for much longer.

The living room was thankfully empty and after being asleep for who knew how long I wasn't even sure where everyone was, but I had other priorities at that moment. Grabbing hold of Ash's arm I dragged her over to the lounge chair and shoved her down in the seat, receiving a disgruntled protest from her in response.

She went to stand again but then stilled at the look I gave her.

I paused to take a few deep breaths before I spoke. "Look, I don't know the details of what happened between you and the guys, and honestly, I don't fucking want to know. All I do know is something happened and you have been avoiding them like the plague for years," I said and watched as she raised her chin stubbornly and looked across the room. I could tell she was trying to shut me out, but I was used to her at this point. I also knew how to get under her skin.

I leaned in closer to her, my voice dropping to a low whisper. "But we are all family, Ash. And family, whether born or made, doesn't run away from each other when things get tough. You need to talk to them, and you need to make things right. Not just for them, but for yourself too."

She looked at me, her eyes narrowing. "And what if I don't want to make things right? What if I'm perfectly happy avoiding them for the rest of my life?"

I shook my head, not buying it for a second. "Don't lie to me, Ash. You love them, and they love you. I can see it every time you look at each other."

She sighed heavily, running a hand through her hair. "I don't know, it's just...complicated."

I nodded in understanding. "I know it's complicated, But avoiding them won't make it any easier. You have to confront the situation and talk things out. You don't have to be best friends again, but you should at least be able to be in the same room without it being awkward."

Ash looked down at her lap, her fingers fidgeting. "I know, but there are some things I haven't told them. Things I haven't told anyone," she said quietly.

I placed a comforting hand on her shoulder. "You don't have to tell them everything all at once. Start with small steps. Just sit down and have a conversation. See where it goes from there."

Ash nodded slowly, seeming to consider my words. "I'll think about it," she said finally.

I smiled, knowing that was the best I was going to get from her at the moment. "That's all I can ask for. Just know that we're all here for you, and we'll support you no matter what."

She looked up at me then, her eyes softening. "Thank you," she said sincerely.

We sat in silence for a few minutes, lost in our thoughts. I couldn't help but worry about what would happen once we left this safe haven.

But I knew that Ash needed to face her past and confront her issues with her family if she ever wanted to move forward. I also knew that I couldn't force her to do anything she wasn't ready for, but I would be there for her every step of the way.

As we sat there in the quiet of the living room, I couldn't help but think about my own past and the things I had to confront in order to become the person I was today. It wasn't easy, but it was necessary for my own growth and well-being.

I hoped that Ash would come to the same realization and take the steps necessary to heal and move forward. But I also knew that it was ultimately her decision, and I would support her no matter what path she chose.

Finally, after what felt like hours, Ash stood up and stretched. "I'm going to go get some fresh air," she said, making her way toward the door. Before she got there the door opened and Kacey walked in. He looked surprised as he almost physically ran into her. It was like the world's most awkward dance as he tried to avoid it.

As Ash left the room, I couldn't help but notice the tension between her and Kacey. It was like watching two cats ready to pounce on each other, and I had a feeling that it wasn't just a chance encounter.

"Awkward much?" I said to Kacey, trying to lighten the mood.

Kacey let out a half-hearted chuckle. "Yeah, you could say that."

I raised an eyebrow. "So, what's going on with you two?"

Kacey sighed. "It's complicated."

I laughed, "Isn't everything," I muttered, the previous conversation with Ash still playing on my mind.

Kacey grimaced. "Yeah, I really don't think I can talk about this with you," he said before wandering off down the hall toward the bedrooms.

I gave a long suffering sigh and let my head fall back on the lounge.

A voice from next to me startled me and I whipped my head up to see Gabe in the entry to the living room. "Ohhh, those two have so fucked and if they haven't they fucking need to."

I groaned, "Please don't talk to me about my sister's sex life."

He laughed loudly in response, "Oh, you mean that wasn't you encouraging her to go back to Nix and the guys even knowing they were panting after her? And that she has one hundred percent fucked Nix?"

I rubbed the heels of my palms into my eyes. "Why me?" I asked and Gabe just continued to laugh.

I looked back at him and decided that I needed to change the topic. "Sorry I was asleep for however long," I said with a grimace.

He shook his head and waved a hand at me. "Nah, you needed it. If it wasn't you in there with her it would have been one of us, but you needed it the most," he said with a grin.

I hummed in acknowledgment. "Are we all set to relocate tomorrow?

He nodded and paused in thought for a moment. "Do you think we will be able to keep her safe there?" he asked.

I thought about it instead of the automatic answer I wanted to give, but then still went with the same answer. "Yes, but either way I want her there. It's our home and I want her there with us. We will just have to make sure we are ready if Dominick does find her there."

He nodded his agreement. "We will be ready for him, no matter what. And we'll make sure she's safe."

I felt a sense of relief hearing his words. We had been through so much already, but we were a team and we would always have each other's back.

We both fell into a comfortable silence, lost in our own thoughts. I couldn't help but worry about what was going to happen next. We were taking a big risk by bringing her back to our home, but I knew it was the right thing to do. We couldn't let Dominick win.

"I'm going to go check on her," I said, standing up from the couch. "You should get some rest too."

He nodded and I made my way down the hallway to her room. As I opened the door, I saw her sleeping fitfully in her bed.

As I sat in the chair next to her bed and took her hand in mine she settled down. I stayed there watching her sleep for a while lost in my thoughts. I couldn't help but think about what the future held for us. But for now, I knew we had to focus on keeping her safe and finding a way to finally put an end to Dominick's reign of terror.

Chapter 15

Alexis

O nce again, I woke up to Colt in the chair by my bed holding my hand. Only this time I had another body pressed to my other side, a tattooed arm wrapped tightly around my stomach but away from the bandages on my ribs. Gabe's face pressed tightly into the side of my neck, restricting the ability for me to move my head in his direction, but I was able to tilt my head enough to spy Rome in the other armchair.

Seeing my movement, Rome stood up from the chair and leaned over Gabe to softly cradle a hand at my face. "Hey, baby girl," he said as he stroked a thumb over my cheekbone.

I smiled softly at him. "Hey," I responded before brushing my lips against his hand.

"I'm sorry I haven't visited sooner, someone decided we weren't allowed to crowd you straight away and that I had to get some sleep first." I could hear the annoyance in his voice as he flicked a frown toward Colt. I glanced in that direction to see Colt was awake and looking back at Rome with a half grin and a raised brow.

I chuckled and the sound seemed to make a smile tug at Rome's lips as he refocused on me. "Your sleep is definitely more important than me."

His fingers grasped my chin tightly. "No. Nothing is more important than you, baby girl. If I hear you talk like that ever again I will turn your ass red."

My eyes widened and I glanced at Colt who also glowered at me. "I'll watch."

I huffed at him before I then heard Gabe mumble into my neck, "Same."

I opened my mouth to argue with them, but even though I obviously couldn't see him from where I was, I should have known Hunt would be there too. "It's unanimous."

I started to try to look around for him only for him to raise himself to his feet against the wall by the bedroom door.

Rome drew my attention back by squeezing my chin again. "Are we clear, baby girl?" he asked.

I nodded, feeling a blush creep up my cheeks. "Crystal clear," I responded softly.

Rome leaned in and pressed a gentle kiss to my forehead before releasing my chin. "Good," he murmured before straightening up. "Now, how are you feeling?"

I took a moment to assess my body, realizing that the pain was still there, but not as intense as before. "Better," I replied honestly, "I do need the toilet though."

Rome's expression softened as he nodded. "Alright, let's get you up then."

Gabe reluctantly released his hold on me, and Rome carefully helped me sit up in the bed. Once I was on my feet, the pain in my ribs flared up again, but I gritted my teeth and tried to ignore it.

After taking care of my needs, I washed my hands and splashed some water on my face before exiting the bathroom.

The men were all still waiting around the room, watching me carefully as I emerged. Rome was the first to speak. "Do you need anything else?" he asked.

I chuckled, "Yeah, to not get back into that bed. I'm done resting now."

The men all exchanged glances before Rome chuckled and shook his head. "You're stubborn as ever, baby girl," he said affectionately. "But alright."

Colt stood up from his chair and stretched. "Well, I don't know about you guys, but I could use some breakfast."

Gabe nodded in agreement. "I could eat," he said.

Colt sent me a grin. "I know of at least one person out there who is desperate to catch up with you, but would you like to have a shower first? Ash grabbed you some clothes and your dressings are waterproof."

I nodded gratefully at Colt. "Yes, please. A shower sounds amazing right now," I said, glancing down at the clothes I was wearing that were far too big for me and obviously belonged to one of the men.

Hunt retrieved a pile of clothes from the bedside table and brought them over to me. "I'll go get started on some breakfast, sweetheart," he said before he pressed a soft kiss to my temple and made his way out of the room.

"We'll go help. Call out if you need us." Colt said before brushing his lips against my cheek and following Hunt. The other two repeated the affection before also trailing out the door.

As I stepped into the shower, the warm water cascaded over me, relaxing my muscles and soothing my sore body. I took my time, enjoying the feeling of the water on my skin and the gentle scent of the body wash.

Once I was finished, I dried off and got dressed in the clothes that Ash brought for me. The bandages were indeed waterproof, so I didn't have to worry about getting them wet.

As I stepped out into the living and dining area, I noticed several people I didn't recognize. I hesitated in the entryway, unsure of where to go or what to do. Suddenly, a feminine shriek broke the silence, causing me to jump in surprise. I saw Ash race towards me, but a body stepped between us, and I instantly recognized Colt's back.

"Ash, no," he growled at her. "She's hurt and has stitches."

I peeked around Colt's back and saw Ash holding her hands up in a placating motion. "Sorry, sorry, I forgot. I'm just excited to see her," she said.

Colt shook his head in exasperation, and I slid past him to embrace Ash. "It's okay, Ash. I'm glad to see you too," I said, smiling at her.

We took a moment to appreciate being together again, I've missed her. But then Colt pulled me back out of her arms and into his.

He pressed a kiss to the side of my head and I saw Ash grin. "Let me introduce you and then I'll grab you some breakfast."

He guided me with his arm as he introduced me to Phoenix, Beckett, and Maverick, his foster brothers. Who I could see from a mile away only had eyes for Ash.

Moving towards the dining area, I stopped in surprise. "Kacey?"

He was leaning against the wall watching everyone. He directed a smile and a nod at me, but I could see that it was strained around the edges. "Hey Lexi, I'm glad you're okay."

I contemplated asking what was wrong, but at that moment Hunt appeared with breakfast for me as Colt directed me to a chair at the dining table. Conversation was a low hum around the room as I slowly ate my food.

Colt turned to me once I had finished. "We are going to move locations later today but there is something that we need to do before we head off though."

I frowned at him in response, confused.

"We need to take care of our guest that Nix has stashed elsewhere," he said.

It dawned on me what he meant. "You still have Enzo?"

I caught the grins of a few of the men around the room. "We kind of thought you might like to get a little revenge." Colt confirmed with a grin tugging at his lips.

I couldn't help but grin back at Colt's words. After everything I had been through this week, I was itching for a chance to get some payback.

"Count me in," I said eagerly.

Colt chuckled. "I thought you might say that."

As we prepared to head out, I noticed Kacey standing off to the side, looking hesitant. I walked over to him and put a hand on his shoulder.

"Hey, you coming with us?" I asked.

He hesitated for a moment before nodding. "Yeah, I'll come. I could use a distraction."

I could tell he was still troubled, but I didn't press him further. Instead, we all piled into a few cars and headed toward the location where Enzo was being held.

Phoenix led us to a small warehouse on the outskirts of town. We all drove into the warehouse and exited the cars, Nix leading us toward a door down a long corridor.

As we approached, Nix motioned for us to be quiet as he opened the door.

Chapter 16

Alexis

Enzo was hanging from a set of chains attached to the wall in a similar fashion to the position I had been in when the men rescued me, but unlike me, Enzo was gagged.

I felt a surge of satisfaction at the sight of him, and I could tell from the looks on the faces of the men around me that they felt the same.

Nix untied the gag from Enzo's mouth, and he looked up at us with a mix of fear and anger in his eyes.

"You're all dead," he spat out.

I stepped forward, my fists clenched at my sides. "No, but you will be soon, Enzo. We have a score to settle first though."

Colt stepped up beside me, a wicked grin on his face.

Enzo looked unimpressed. "You think this is going to scare me? You think I'm going to beg for mercy?"

I laughed which startled him, his expression faltered for a moment before he sneered at me.

"I don't need you to beg for mercy, Enzo," I said with a smirk. "I just need you to hurt the way you and Nick like to hurt others."

I looked around the room to see the men had spread out around the walls watching, allowing me to have my moment. Only Colt was by my side to offer support.

Enzo scoffed. "You don't have the guts to do anything to me."

I stepped closer to him, my eyes locked on his. "I told you before you would regret underestimating me, Enzo."

With that, I punched him hard in the stomach, causing him to gasp for air. The sound of his chains rattling filled the room as he tried to catch his breath.

Enzo snarled at me. "You have no idea what you're dealing with. You're just a little girl playing in a man's world."

I took a step closer to him, narrowing my eyes. "I may be a girl, Enzo, but I'm not little and I'm not afraid of you. You're just a coward who gets off on hurting people weaker than yourself."

I could see Enzo's anger boiling over as he struggled against the chains holding him up. But I didn't back down. I stood my ground, ready to make him pay for what he had done to me and to others.

Enzo gritted out. "You're not going to get anything out of me."

"Maybe not," I replied. "After all, I'm just a little girl playing in a man's world." I looked around at the men in the room. "These men's world to be exact. And since they do want information from you, I'm not going to tell them right now exactly what you said to me, what you did to me, what you threatened to do to me."

Enzo's expression changed, his eyes widened with the re-alization of his mistake. He had underestimated me, and now he was paying for it.

I continued, "But don't worry, Enzo. We have ways of get-ting what we want. And when we're done with you, you won't be able to hurt anyone again."

Colt stepped forward, his hand gripping Enzo's chin rough-ly, forcing him to look him in the eyes. "You better start talking, Enzo. And fast. Because if you don't, you're going to regret it even more than you already do."

"I don't know anything," he said, his voice hoarse.

I raised an eyebrow. "Really? Because I find that hard to believe. You and Nick have been running this operation for years. You were obviously the one in charge while Nick was in prison. You must have some information that's useful to us."

Enzo remained silent, his jaw clenched.

I sighed. "Fine. You leave me no choice." I turned to the men in the room. "Gentlemen, do what you have to do."

The men nodded, and I stepped back as they closed in on Enzo. Colt gripped my shoulder, "You don't have to stay if you don't want to."

I shook my head in response. "I need to," I confessed.

I watched as they began to work him over, the sounds echoing around the room of fists hitting flesh, bones crack-ing, and Enzo's screams of pain. It was a brutal scene, but I knew it was necessary if we were going to get the information we needed.

After what seemed like an eternity, the men finally stopped. Enzo was barely conscious, his face a bloody mess. But he was still alive. And he still refused to break.

I walked over to him and looked him in the eye. "You're a stubborn asshole aren't you?" I asked softly.

Enzo spat out a mouthful of blood. "Go to hell," he muttered.

Nix indicated for Colt and I to speak to him on the other side of the room, next to a table of torture tools, while he used a cloth to wipe some of the blood from his hands and arms.

Colt brushed a hand down my arm in a discreet show of comfort as we made our way across the room to talk to him.

"He isn't going to budge. He will happily take his secrets to the grave with him." Nix confirmed what I already knew. It was worth a try though.

I hummed as I nodded in agreement, my eyes landing on the tools at Nix's side. I picked up a long sharp looking knife and turned back towards Enzo.

"Lexi?" Colt asked as I walked away from them and to the man hanging from chains.

I brought the knife up to look at it in the light, and watched as Enzo's eyes widened.

"What was it that you said to me again, Enzo? You were going to make me scream right? That you were going to cut me and fuck me until I was nothing but a whimpering, broken mess. And then, you would make sure I begged for death." I recalled aloud.

I heard several growls and the scuffle of bodies behind me but my focus was completely on the man in front of me.

I didn't give myself another moment to think about it before I plunged the knife into his groin. He shrieked again and again, the sound sharp and echoing. I pulled the knife back out to another scream from him and watched as the blood joined the pools of it already on the floor. I brought the knife up again to stab him in the chest but a hand wrapped around my wrist.

I looked up at Hunt who had stopped me.

"Let us, sweetheart. It won't be our first kill or our last. You don't need to taint your soul on a piece of garbage like him," he said softly, his hand moving up to gently pull the knife from my hand.

I nodded in acknowledgment and glanced back at the others in the room. Colt's brothers were restraining Colt, Gabe, and Rome who must have reacted badly to what Enzo had said.

The sound of a gunshot startled me and I quickly turned back to see Hunt's gun aimed at the now dead Enzo. I reached out and gently touched his arm holding the gun and Hunt lowered his arm to turn towards me. He reached out and dragged me into his body, wrapping himself around me, his nose pressing into my hair breathing me in.

Nix approached while we stood there holding each other. "We will clean this up, you guys head out, you have a long drive."

I felt Hunt nod against me and he turned us towards the door. Ash stopped us on the way out the door and gave me a hug, making me and Colt promise to get in touch as soon as we could.

We made our way to the vehicle and after climbing in the back with Hunt and Gabe, while Colt climbed into the driver's seat and Rome got into the passenger seat, we left the warehouse in silence, the weight of what had just happened settling heavily on all of us. Hunt's grip on me was tight as we drove, his thumb tracing patterns on the back of my hand. I knew he was processing everything that had happened, and I was doing the same. The adrenaline started to wear off and my body began to shake. Hunt noticed and pulled me closer to him, rubbing my back soothingly. We drove for what felt like hours before finally pulling into the driveway of a house.

A stunning house.

"Welcome home, princess." Colt breathed from the driver's seat as we pulled into the garage.

I looked around as best I could from my position. "Is this another safe house?"

Rome looked back at me from the passenger seat. "No, this is our home."

Chapter 17

Alexis

I felt a sense of déjà vu as Hunt led me from the car and into the house, only this time the other men were following closely behind us. It was a large ranch style home with high ceilings and a lot of windows. The interior was light and modern and such a vast difference from the safe house that I breathed a sigh of relief.

Hunt didn't show me around this time, as we all came to stand near the dining table and the men offloaded bags of weapons and then stood for a moment.

A sense of dread crept into me as I took in their serious expressions.

Colt moved closer to me, and brushed his knuckles against my cheek. "Princess, we aren't going to ask you to relive what you went through right now, but you will need to talk about it someday to someone," he started and I looked down at the table, taking controlled breaths.

Hunt reached out and took one of my hands in his, giving it a reassuring squeeze until I focused on Colt again.

Anger flashed across his face but I knew it wasn't directed at me. "Remember when I said we would wait and let the FBI deal with that asshole?"

I nodded in response. "Yeah?"

"Well, fuck that shit. We are no longer sitting back and waiting. For what he did to you, he dies at our hands. The moment he touched you again he signed his own death warrant."

I could see the others nodding in agreement and my heart clenched in my chest at his words. If I didn't know I was falling for them before, I certainly did now. Emotions I didn't want to assess just yet were raging inside of me.

"But for the moment let's leave that discussion and a tour until tomorrow," he said as he held his hands out to me. "We all need a shower and sleep, it's been a long messy day. Let me help you, princess."

I placed my hands in his. He waited while the others gently kissed me before he pulled me behind him, leading me through the house and up a set of stairs, making his way into a bedroom that must have been his. It's all masculine colors and a simplistic design. He kept walking, taking me into an attached ensuite. He reached into the shower and turned it on before he turned towards me and slowly helped me strip out of my dirty, blood stained clothes.

He was silent as he stripped us down and moved me under the warm water, gently starting to clean me and wash all the dirt and blood from my skin and hair. He was careful not to touch any intimate areas more than necessary.

As he washed me, I couldn't help but feel a sense of safety and comfort with him. His touch was gentle yet firm, and he seemed to know exactly what he was doing. I closed my eyes and let the warm water cascade over me, feeling the tension slowly ebb away.

The events of the day were still fresh in my mind, but being here with him made everything feel a little bit easier. I let out a contented sigh as he ran his fingers through my hair, massaging my scalp as he rinsed the shampoo out.

Once he was done washing me, he washed himself then turned off the water and pulled me from the shower. Grabbing a fluffy towel from a cupboard, he softly dried me off before he lifted me to sit on the bathroom counter. He pulled off the bandages across my ribs and using a first aid kit he retrieved from the same cupboard as the towels, he cleaned the stitches and redressed the wounds.

He then lifted me from the counter again and cradled me to him as I wrapped my legs around him. He carried me to his bed, sliding us under the covers together with me curled onto his chest.

He was still silent, not having said anything since we entered the room and I was starting to worry. I lifted my head to look at him, trying to read the expression on his face. It was clear that he was deep in thought, his brow furrowed in a frown. A wave of concern washed over me, and I found myself whispering to him, not wanting to disturb the fragile calm he had created.

"What's wrong?" I asked softly, my eyes searching his face.

His eyes met mine, and for a moment, he seemed lost in his own thoughts. His frown deepened, and I could see the worry etched on his face. "Nothing, princess," he said finally, his voice low and gentle. "Get some rest."

I sat up a little straighter, my gaze still locked on his face. "Don't do that," I pleaded with him. "Don't shut me out."

He took a deep breath before speaking again, his voice tinged with self-doubt. "I failed you," he admitted. "I was meant to keep you safe, and I didn't."

I shook my head, feeling a surge of emotion. "You were injured," I reminded him. "I thought they had killed you. And yet, you still came for me."

He looked at me with a seriousness that I felt deep in my bones. "I would die for you," he said.

I smiled at him softly, feeling a warmth spread through my chest. "I don't need you to die for me," I said. "I need you to live for me."

"I do live for you," he said, his voice filled with conviction. "Every fiber of my being lives and longs for you. The breath I breathe is for you."

My heart swelled at his words, and I found myself leaning toward him. "Then show me, Colt," I whispered. "Show me how much you want me."

He looked at me, his eyes darkening with desire. "How?" he asked, his voice thick with emotion.

"Touch me," I said, my own voice trembling. "Make me yours again."

He nodded slowly, his hand reaching out to brush a strand of hair from my face. I shivered at his touch, feeling a jolt of electricity run through my body. He leaned up, his lips meeting mine in a slow and gentle kiss. Our bodies pressed together.

With practiced ease, he rolled us over, his body now hovering over mine. His hands roamed over my skin avoiding my injuries, tracing the curves of my body, and igniting a fire within me. I moaned softly as he kissed his way down my neck, his lips leaving a trail of heat in their wake.

As he reached my breasts, he took a nipple into his mouth, sucking and nibbling on it until I was writhing beneath him. His other hand worked its way down between my legs, finding the wetness there and sliding a finger inside me. I gasped at the sensation, my body arching towards him in response.

He added a second finger, slowly pumping them in and out of me as he continued to suck on my nipple. I was lost in a haze of pleasure, my body humming with desire. I reached for him, pulling him closer to me and urging him on.

He complied eagerly, his fingers curling inside me, driving me toward the edge of ecstasy. His mouth left my breast, and I felt a pang of loss until his lips found their way to mine once more, his tongue probing and teasing me. I responded eagerly, my own tongue tangling with his as I rocked my hips on his fingers.

He shifted his weight, moving down my body again until his face was level with my pussy. He looked up at me, his eyes hooded and smoldering with desire, before he slowly lowered his mouth to me, sliding his tongue from where his fingers continued to move inside me to circle around my throbbing clit. I cried out as he closed his mouth over it, his tongue flicking while his mouth sucked gently.

He continued to alternate between licking and gently sucking on me with his mouth while he continued thrusting and moving his fingers, the sensations building within me until with a cry, I shattered into a million pieces, my body convulsing with pleasure. He rode out my orgasm with me, never once letting up until I collapsed bonelessly beneath him.

Pulling his fingers from me he gave my sensitive pussy a few soft licks before sucking his fingers into his mouth to clean them off. He crawled up my body, and his lips found mine once more. We kissed slowly and deeply, savoring the taste of each other.

He rolled us again until I straddled his waist, my hands running over his chest and down his abdomen. I could feel his hardness pressing against me, and I wanted nothing more than to feel him inside me once again.

"Ride me, princess. I need to feel you wrapped around my cock again, I miss your pussy," he growled out softly.

I reached down, wrapping my hand around his length and stroking him slowly. He groaned, his head falling back as he surrendered to the pleasure I was giving him. I positioned myself over him, slowly lowering myself down onto him. We both moaned at the sensation, our bodies coming together once again.

I started moving my hips, riding him with a slow and steady rhythm. He reached out and gripped my hips, controlling my movements as we both lost ourselves in the pleasure of the moment. Our bodies moved together as one, the intensity building with each passing second.

I leaned back, gripping his thighs as he continued to slowly rock my hips back and forth; he filled me completely, and I felt him deep inside me as we moved. My eyes closed as my head fell back, lost in the pleasure he was giving me.

I felt him rise to sit up, his chest pressed to mine as one of his arms left my hip to grip the back of my neck, bringing my head up to look at him. "Eyes on me, princess," he growled as he rested his forehead against mine and my hands moved to wrap around his neck. My eyes locked onto his as we continued to move together. The intensity between us grew with each passing moment, the pleasure building and building until it was almost too much to bear.

I felt his breath on my lips as he leaned in, his mouth claiming mine in a fierce kiss. Our tongues danced together, each of us surrendering to the passion we shared. I moaned into the kiss, my hands gripping his shoulders as I lost myself in the sensation of his mouth on mine and his cock deep inside me.

I broke away from the kiss, gasping for breath as I continued to ride him. He buried his face in my neck, his teeth grazing my skin as he bit down gently.

I let out a gasp of pleasure, my hands gripping his hair as he continued to kiss and nip at my neck. The sensation was almost too much, the pleasure building inside of me until I was on the brink of another orgasm.

He could sense my impending climax and began to thrust up into me with more force and urgency. Our bodies moved together and our moans and gasps filled the air around us.

And then it hit me, a wave of pleasure so intense that it felt like my entire body was exploding. I cried out his name as I came, my body convulsing with the force of my orgasm. He followed right behind me, his cum filling me as my pussy clenched around him.

We stayed wrapped around each other, both of us panting and sweating as we tried to catch our breath. In that moment,

I knew that I was completely and utterly theirs, and that there was no going back.

Chapter 18

Alexis

Dawn found me tangled with Colt and him still fast asleep. It wasn't often I got to see him truly asleep so I took a moment to appreciate the sight. He hadn't shaved since I had been taken and his beard was now starting to rival his brother Nix's, not that I was complaining after the extra stimulation it helped create the previous night.

Sliding as gently as I could from the bed I stole a loose shirt from his closet that looked long enough to pass for a short dress and then snuck into the ensuite for a quick shower. I was feeling a lot better now and was even able to look at myself in the mirror without cringing too badly at the fading scrapes and bruises.

Leaving the bathroom I saw that Colt had rolled onto his stomach, cuddling my abandoned pillow as though it were me, bringing a small smile to my lips as I slipped out of the bedroom.

I wandered down the stairs to the main living area, taking in the details that I had missed yesterday in my distraction.

The living room was spacious with high ceilings and large windows that allowed for plenty of natural light to flood in. The furniture was a mix of leather and plush fabrics in neutral colors, giving the space a cozy yet sophisticated feel. A large stone fireplace dominated one wall, with a thick rug in front of it and a few comfortable armchairs arranged around it.

I moved towards the kitchen, which was just as impressive as the rest of the house. It had a large island in the center with bar stools placed around it, and high end appliances. Everything looked clean and new, which made me wonder how often they actually used it.

I could smell the faint scent of coffee, which made me realize how much I needed a cup. I found the coffee maker and brewed a pot, enjoying the aroma as it filled the air.

As I sipped my coffee I checked the cupboards and fridge and got to work preparing breakfast for everyone.

Lost in my thoughts, I didn't hear when someone snuck up behind me until they wrapped their arms around me from behind, careful to avoid where he knew my stitches were, causing me to jump.

"Good morning, beautiful," Gabe said, pressing a kiss to the back of my neck.

I relaxed into his embrace, taking a moment to enjoy the feeling of being in his arms again. "Good morning to you too," I replied, turning around to face him.

His hands found my waist as he leaned forward to brush his lips against mine.

"Careful or breakfast will burn." Hunt said as he slid past us and towards the coffee pot. I gasped and turned around, moving the food around in the pan again.

Gabe chuckled and moved me out of the way and in the direction of his brother as he took over the cooking for me, ignoring my protests.

Hunt put a freshly poured coffee on the bench near Gabe before he drew me into his arms, kissing me slowly and deeply until I was panting. Then he released me in order to pour his own coffee. I leaned heavily against the kitchen counter, trying to regain my composure.

I heard a noise by the entry to the kitchen and turned to see Colt standing in the doorway. He was shirtless, his hair still damp from the shower, and the burning desire that I had just managed to tame came roaring back to life. Seriously, these men were trying to set my non-existent panties on fire.

"Good morning, princess," he said, his voice low and rough. "Sleep well?"

I nodded, and I could feel the heat spread across my cheeks again. "Yeah, I did. Thanks."

He walked over to me, his eyes taking in my outfit. "You look good in my shirt," he said, a hint of a smile on his lips.

I ducked my head, knowing that my face was now flaming. "Thanks. I didn't have anything else to wear."

He chuckled. "It looks better on you than it does on me."

He tilted my chin up with a finger before brushing his lips against mine before he too moved over to the coffee pot.

"This is cozy." Rome's voice was nothing but humor as he also entered the kitchen. It was a good thing it was such a large room since there were so many of us. Hunt moved to help Gabe with breakfast, moving around me effortlessly while Colt pulled up a seat at the kitchen island.

Rome wandered over to also give me a soft kiss and for a moment I wondered if I was still dreaming. He used my hand to pull me out of the way of Gabe and Hunt and around to one of the stools at the island between him and Colt.

As we all sat down to eat, the conversation flowed easily between us. We chatted about inconsequential things, laughing and joking as though we didn't have a care in the world. It was a surreal moment, one that I knew wouldn't last forever, but I cherished it nonetheless. I couldn't help but feel grateful to be surrounded by these amazing men who risked so much to save me.

As we finished eating, I could sense the atmosphere getting slightly tense and I knew that we needed to have some serious conversations.

Colt looked at me seriously, taking a moment to think about how he wanted to word what he wanted to say. "We aren't hiding anymore. You aren't going to hide anymore."

I nodded, knowing that it was time for me to face the reality of the situation. "I know. I'm ready. I want him gone, I can face him."

They frown at me. "We aren't letting you go after him alone." Colt said.

I scoffed. "Jeez, give me some credit. I'm not that self-sacrificing."

They all look at me with a frown as though I've highly offended them.

I shrugged and said, "What? I know my strengths and weaknesses. We work better as a team so we will plan and take down this asshole as a team."

A soft look briefly passed over Colt's face.

Hunt spoke up next. "We need to figure out a plan. We can't just sit here and wait for him to come after you."

Gabe agreed. "We need to be proactive. We need to take the fight to him."

Rome added his thoughts. "But we need to be careful. We don't know who we can trust."

I nodded in agreement, knowing that they were all right. "So what's the plan?"

They looked at each other, silently communicating before Hunt spoke up. "We need to gather as much information as we can."

Rome nodded. "And we need to strengthen our defenses. We can't let him catch us off guard again."

Colt stood up, his eyes blazing with determination. "And we need to make it clear to him that he's not going to win. That he's not going to take you away from us again."

I nodded in agreement with him, "As I said, I'm ready now, let him try to come for me."

"We are not using you as bait." Gabe growled.

I laughed at him. "I think we can establish I'm no one's bait, I'm the hook. Let that asshole come and try to get to me again— I'll tear his fucking throat out."

Chapter 19

Alexis

After our conversation over breakfast, Colt and Rome left to take care of some work tasks that they neglected, while Gabe and Hunt decided that they would take me out to buy some clothes since I had none.

When I hesitated, they explained that we wanted my presence out in public so it would potentially bring Nick to us.

Hunt supplied me with some pants to wear and even though they were tightened as much as possible they were still too big.

He also tried to give me a new gun to replace the one from the safe house, but until I had somewhere to put it I couldn't carry it with me. He reassured me that they would all still have at least one weapon on them at all times.

As they drove me to the local mall, we relaxed and bantered and joked between us, falling back into the comfortable connection we had before.

Once we arrived at the mall, Gabe and Hunt led me to the first clothing store we came across. They both immediately began scouring the racks for clothes that would fit me.

As they picked out clothes, they asked me about my style and what I liked to wear. I told them I didn't really have a style since I never really owned much clothing before, always keeping only to the essentials in case I needed to run.

Gabe and Hunt then took it upon themselves to help me find a style that I liked. They suggested different outfits for me to try on, and I was surprised at how much I enjoyed the experience.

We entered another high end clothing store and were instantly greeted by a tall leggy blonde. It certainly wasn't lost on me that she was wanting to help and please the guys and not me. We were walking around picking clothes out when the blond bitch giggled and ran her hand along Gabe's arm for what felt like the millionth time.

I turned to snap at her but was dragged away by Hunt to try on the clothes he piled into the spacious changing room. Moments later there was a knock on the changing room door and when I opened it Gabe was standing in the doorway with a grin, passing some lingerie to me. I narrowed my eyes. "Really?" I asked.

Gabe smirked, his eyes roaming over my body. "Oh, definitely. You have the perfect body for lingerie," he said, his voice low and husky.

I rolled my eyes and closed the door, eyeing the pieces of lace on their hangers. I pulled off the dress I tried on and slipped into the lingerie, my fingers trailing slowly along the lace covering one of my breasts as I looked at myself in the mirror. The way the lingerie wrapped around my body and cupped my breasts meant you could barely even see the dressings across my ribs, the matching g-string was high cut and showed off my toned stomach and hips.

I never invested in anything like this— I always considered the expense frivolous.

Stepping closer to the mirror, I let my hand trail down my body, looking at myself as my hand moved slowly down the lace.

I heard a noise behind me and looked up to see the reflection of two burning pairs of light blue eyes as Gabe and Hunt took in the sight of me.

Gabe turned the lock behind him as Hunt moved towards me like a hungry wolf.

My heart rate quickened as Hunt stepped closer, his eyes never leaving my body. I felt a shiver run down my spine as he reached out and traced his finger along the lace, his touch sending a jolt of electricity through me.

Gabe stepped closer too, his eyes smoldering with desire. "You look incredible," he said, his voice low and rough, his fingers lightly brushing over the strap on my shoulder.

I bit my lip, feeling a flush creeping up my neck.

Hunt leaned in, his lips grazing my neck as he whispered, "Do you realize how sexy you are?"

I shuddered at his touch, my body responding to his words. I felt a surge of heat as their touch sent electric sparks through my body. My breath quickened as I went to turn to face them, but Hunt held me in place facing the mirror.

Hunt leaned in, his lips brushing against my ear, "You know, we can't resist you when you look like this," he whispered.

Gabe's fingers trailed down my lace covered breast, tracing the curve. "We want to make you feel good, beautiful," he murmured.

My knees felt weak as their words and touches ignited a fire inside me. I looked up at them, my eyes filled with desire.

"Then make me feel good," I whispered, my voice husky.

It was so easy to be in the moment with them, to forget about everything that had happened and just feel what they made me feel. They made the world outside disappear.

Gabe's lips connected with my neck, and I let out a moan as Hunt's fingers trailed down my body, their touches sending shivers through me. My eyes followed the path of Hunt's fingers as they reached the lace edges of the g-string.

"Let's show the blond Barbie out there who I really belong to," Gabe whispered in my ear before licking and nipping at it. I was panting with desire, and there was no way this lingerie was going back on the shelf. His lips moved back to my neck, kissing and nipping at the sensitive skin as his hand cupped my breast closest to him. His tongue piercing pressed into my skin as he placed open mouthed kisses there. My body arched into his touch, a low whimper escaping my lips as my eyes fell shut.

Hunt's fingers slipped beneath the waistband of the g-string, and I gasped as they slid slowly through my wetness and directly into my drenched pussy.

Gabe tugged at the lace covering my breast, pulling it aside to reveal my hard nipple. His mouth closed over it, sucking and flicking the metal ball in his mouth against the sensitive peak until I arched into his touch.

My fingers tangled in their hair, pulling them closer as I lost myself in the sensations. The heat between us was palpable, and I could feel myself getting wetter with desire with every lick, nip, suck and movement. I felt myself getting closer to the edge, the pleasure building inside me until I was trembling with need.

Hunt's hand gripped my hair tightly, moving my head where he wanted it, his hot breath feathering against my ear as he leaned close and his other hand continued to thrust his fingers into me.

"Open your eyes, sweetheart. I want you to watch every second as we make you cum," he whispered huskily into my ear. "And then you're going to take our cocks like a good girl. I want you walking out of this store dripping in our cum."

I opened my eyes, watching as Hunt's fingers plunged in and out of me, the wet sounds echoing in the small space. Gabe's mouth was still on my breast, his teeth grazing my nipple, sending waves of pleasure through me.

I felt the tension building inside me, the pleasure almost unbearable as I felt myself getting closer and closer to the edge. Hunt's fingers curled inside me, hitting just the right spot, and I cried out as the orgasm ripped through me, my body shaking with the force of it.

As I came down from the high, I felt Hunt pull his fingers out of me and watched as he licked them clean, a satisfied smile on his face. Gabe's mouth moved up my neck, leaving a trail of kisses as he whispered, "You're so fucking sexy." His hands gripped my waist as Hunt moved away briefly, moving back moments later after pulling the bench seat closer. He undid his pants before sitting down on the bench, releasing his throbbing cock as he did. He reached out and pulled me back towards him as Gabe helped me straddle Hunt's lap until I was sitting facing the mirror with my legs over the outside of Hunt's. They worked together to raise me back up and move the lingerie aside and then I was slowly sinking onto Hunt's cock.

Hunt spread our combined legs wide and I could see every detail in the mirror as it disappeared into my pussy, only adding to the feeling of it stretching me. I gasped as Hunt's cock filled me up completely, my walls clenching around him as I started to ride him slowly. Hunt's hands moved to my breasts, squeezing and teasing my nipples as I moved up and down on his length. One of his hands traveled up to circle my throat, squeezing and dragging my head back to rasp into my ear, "Look how pretty that pussy is taking my cock. You like watching my cock inside you, don't you sweetheart? I can feel you squeezing me so tight. You're such a good fucking girl, taking every inch of me." His words sent shivers down my spine as I continued to ride him, feeling my pleasure build with each movement.

Hunt's voice was thick with desire as he continued to praise me, his words sending a fresh wave of arousal through me. "I love how you look when you're being fucked. You're so fucking beautiful, sweetheart," he said, his hand squeezed my throat harder and my hands automatically came up to grip his wrist. "Your pussy is so fucking wet for me. You need our cocks, don't you? You can't get enough of them," he growled, his eyes locking onto mine in the mirror as he thrust into me harder.

I moaned in response, my body responding eagerly to his every touch and words. "Yes, please fuck me harder. I need you." I begged, my nails digging into his skin.

Gabe stepped closer in front of me, standing between our legs as he released his cock from his pants. His hand fisted his throbbing cock, giving it a few strokes before he gripped a handful of my hair. His piercing glinted in the overhead light. "Open that sexy mouth for me, beautiful, and swallow my cock."

Hunt released my throat and I instantly complied, leaning forward I flicked the piercing at the end of his cock with my tongue before I took his entire length deep into my mouth. Gabe groaned as I swallowed around him, my tongue swirling around his cock as I bobbed my head up and down. His grip tightened in my hair as he thrust his hips forward, pushing himself into my throat until his cock piercing scraped against it. I moaned, the sensation of being filled by both of them driving me wild.

Hunt's hands moved to my hips, guiding me faster and harder on his cock, his own soft moans filling the air. "Your pussy feels so fucking good," Hunt groaned.

The pleasure that was building inside me was aching to be released. I could feel Hunt getting closer as he thrust deeper and harder into me, his hands squeezing my hips tighter. Hunt released one of my hips to slide his hand down my body and back into the lace g-string, and I moaned around Gabe's cock as Hunt's thumb brushed against my clit.

My eyes were fixed on the mirror as I watched the three of us moving together in perfect harmony. I could see the pleasure etched on their faces and the way their eyes were glued to my body as I moved.

My whimpers turned into loud moans as the edge approached rapidly. Hunt's dirty talk was fueling my desire, his cock felt like it was hitting every sweet spot inside me, and I knew that I wouldn't be able to hold on much longer.

Hunt's fingers dug into my skin as he pinched my clit, his words sending me over the edge. "Cum for us, sweetheart. Scream so loud that the whole world can hear how good we're making you feel," he growled in my ear.

As my orgasm hit me hard, I screamed around Gabe's cock, my body shaking uncontrollably as I shattered into a million pieces. My walls clenched around Hunt's cock, squeezing him hard as he continued to thrust into me with a relentless intensity. With a deep, primal groan, Hunt tensed beneath me, his body erupting with hot streams of cum as he filled me up.

Gabe pulled himself out of my mouth with lightning speed, and I became aware that he hadn't climaxed yet. He lifted me up and spun me around so that I was facing Hunt, and pushed me forward onto Hunt's thighs.

"Get ready, beautiful, this might get a little rough," Gabe rasped, his hands gripping my hips tightly as he thrust into me hard.

My body jerked forward from the force, and I let out a moan of pleasure. Gabe's thrusts were adding to the intense pleasure that was still coursing through my body from my previous orgasm, his piercing hitting the end of me and scraping against me with each thrust of his hips. I could feel my walls fluttering around him, urging him on as he pounded into me with reckless abandon.

The heat was building inside me again, and my body responded eagerly to the relentless assault of Gabe's cock.

But it was Hunt's eyes that held me captive, the hunger and desire burning in them fueling my own lust. One of his hands grabbed the back of my neck while the other circled my throat, and he leaned forward, his lips brushing against my ear as he whispered, "That's it, take his cock like a good fucking girl."

The words sent shivers down my spine, and I knew I was close. My body was on fire, every nerve ending screaming with pleasure. He pressed his lips to mine in a feverish kiss. Our tongues tangled together, exploring each other's mouths as the pleasure intensified.

The sensation was almost too much to bear, but I couldn't help but love every moment of it. The way Gabe's hips met mine with a loud smack, the way Hunt's hands squeezed gently and made my breath stutter, and the way my body was being used for their pleasure.

My mind was clouded with lust and desire, and I lost all sense of time and space. I was lost in a sea of sensations, and I didn't want it to end. But eventually, my body couldn't take it anymore, and I felt myself approaching the edge again.

"Please, please, please," I chanted, begging for release. Gabe's thrusts were becoming harder and more erratic, and I knew he was close too.

"Fuck, you feel so good, beautiful," Gabe growled, his hands gripping my hips so tightly it left bruises. "You like that, huh?"

"Yes, yes, yes," I moaned, unable to form any coherent words. The pleasure was too much, too overwhelming.

Hunt was watching us with an intensity that made my stomach clench. "Look at you, taking my brother's cock so well," he said, his voice rough with desire. "You're so fucking hot."

"Cum with me, beautiful," Gabe groaned, and with one final thrust, he sent me over the edge. My body convulsed around him, and I moaned as I came hard, my nails digging into his legs.

Gabe followed soon after, filling me up with his own release. We collapsed onto the floor, panting and gasping for air, our bodies slick with sweat and pleasure, my head rested against Hunt's leg.

We stayed like that for a few moments, catching our breaths and basking in the afterglow of our intense experience. Hunt's fingers gently trailed softly through my hair as we sat there.

He turned to Gabe and arched an eyebrow. "So, do they have this lingerie set in any other color?"

It's said with such seriousness that I couldn't help but laugh. Gabe groaned as I stood up, moving me off his cock.

Our combined releases slid down my leg as they watched while Hunt groaned again. "Fuck, that's hot," he murmured.

I chuckled as I turned away from him and placed my hands on my hips to look at myself in the mirror, also watching them watch me as I did it. "You're right, it is hot, we definitely need to see if they have it in other colors."

They grinned at me before Hunt leaned forward to slap my bare ass cheek.

I retrieved a pair of pants and loose top from the pile of clothes I liked and pulled them over the ruined lingerie as they tucked themselves away. Handing Gabe the tags from the clothes I moved out of the changing room with Hunt following close behind, raising an eyebrow at the blond store assistant with her flaming red cheeks who avoided looking at either of us as we moved to wait for Gabe to finalize the purchases.

Turned out they did have it in other colors according to a smirking Gabe.

Chapter 20

Rome

Being back in our own home was surreal. Having Lexi there with us was even more surreal.

But fuck it felt good.

While the twins took her to get some clothes and whatever other items she needed, Colt and I needed to get some work and planning done. Our jobs were piling up and although he was reallocating them to other teams we often worked with, it was starting to get increasingly difficult.

At the same time, we needed to come up with a plan to lure Dominick out, only when he was gone would we truly know that Lexi was safe and we could have our happy ending. If she would have us that was. If she would feel for us the way we were starting to feel for her.

As we sat at the kitchen table, I opened up my laptop and started to go through the various tasks that needed to be done. Colt was pacing around the room, his mind seemingly lost in thought. I knew he was just as worried as I was about Lexi's safety.

But then Colt let out a heavy sigh and paused his pacing. "Do you think she's okay?" he asked me, his voice quiet.

I looked up from my laptop and met his eyes. "I hope so," I replied honestly. "But we can't be sure until we get Dominick out of the picture."

Colt nodded slowly, then resumed his pacing again. I returned my attention to my laptop, but I couldn't help the nagging worry in the back of my mind. Lexi was a strong, capable woman, but she'd been through so much. I didn't know how much more she could take.

"We need to focus," I said, trying to break the silence. "We can't let our emotions get in the way of getting things done."

"I know, I know," Colt replied, rubbing his hands over his face. "It's just hard, you know? Knowing that she's been through so much and we can't do anything about it."

"I know. But we have to keep our heads in the game. We need to come up with a plan to lure Dominick out."

Colt nodded and sat down at the table. "Okay, let's brainstorm. What are our options? We know he's somehow keeping a close eye on her, he always knows where she is. I put it down to the leaks in Kacey's team the first time but there was no way he should have found that safe house."

I nodded. "We need to catch his attention. We need to give him some hope that he could get to her again. To somehow think he would be able to take her from us like last time."

He looked deep in thought for a few moments. "Lexi is right, she is the hook. Everyone has spent all this time keeping her safe and trying to hide her when in reality he is always going to hunt her down whether she hides or not. So maybe we do the opposite."

I frowned. "What do you mean?"

"Lexi said she doesn't want to hide anymore, so let's not hide her. Let's actively *not* hide her," he said.

I shook my head. "That's still essentially using her as bait. I don't like the idea of using her as bait."

"No, not bait, just not hiding. We make sure at least two of us are with her at all times if we go out and we always stay armed and vested but we live our lives, she lives her life, like normal."

I considered Colt's idea for a moment. It did make sense in a way, to not hide Lexi but also not make it obvious that she was being protected. It could possibly lure Dominick out, thinking that he had an opportunity to take her again. But it still felt risky to me.

"I see what you're saying," I said slowly. "But it's still a risk. We don't know how Dominick will react or what he's capable of. We have to make sure Lexi is safe at all times."

"I know," Colt said, rubbing his hands along the scruff of his beard. "But we can't keep her locked up forever. And if we keep hiding her, he's going to keep finding her. We need to change the game."

I nodded, seeing his point. We couldn't keep doing the same thing and expect a different outcome. We needed to take a different approach if we wanted to get rid of Dominick for good.

"Okay," I said finally. "Let's do it. But we need to be cautious and have a plan in case something goes wrong."

"Agreed," Colt said. "We'll need to have a system in place for who's with her at all times and what to do if something happens."

I nodded in agreement. "And we'll need to communicate this plan with Lexi so that she's aware of everything and can be prepared if something were to happen."

Colt leaned forward, his eyes intense. "We'll do whatever it takes to keep her safe, no matter what. We can't let her go through what she went through before."

I could hear the determination in his voice, and it matched my own. We were going to do everything in our power to keep Lexi safe and finally bring an end to Dominick's reign of terror.

We spent the rest of the afternoon planning and strategizing, coming up with a detailed plan to keep Lexi safe while also trying to lure Dominick out. It was risky, but it was the only option we had left.

When Lexi returned with the twins, we sat her down and explained the plan to her. She listened carefully, asking questions and offering suggestions. We could tell she was nervous, but also relieved to finally have a plan in place.

It was our best chance at luring Dominick out and finally putting an end to this nightmare.

As the night wore on, we finally finished our work and were able to relax for a moment. Lexi had already gone to bed, curled up between the twins in Hunt's room, exhausted from the events of the day.

I set up one of the screens on my desk to access the camera for that room and watched her sleep for a moment. She looked so beautiful without the stresses of the situation on her mind. But then she looked beautiful no matter what. I couldn't help but feel a sense of protectiveness towards her as she slept, knowing that we were taking a huge risk by implementing this plan.

But I also knew that we were doing the right thing. We couldn't keep hiding and running forever. We needed to take control of the situation and fight back. I was ready for whatever was to come.

Diverting my attention away from her sleeping form I pulled up a saved video on my screen from my secure storage, thankful I had saved it before my laptop had been destroyed. Turning the volume up on my laptop the sounds of her soft whimpers and moans filled the air around me. I closed my eyes and took a moment to immerse myself in the sound, leaning back in my chair and letting my head rest against the headrest.

"Do you want this, baby girl? Do you want me to be buried deep inside you?"

"Yes, Sir."

My cock was already hard at the first breathy echo of her voice. My mind was already playing back the whole scene in front of me in graphic detail without even looking at the video. I undid my pants and shoved them down, moving to grasp my hard cock tightly in my hand.

"Beg for it."

"Please, Sir. I need you inside me."

I groaned as my cock throbbed, my fingers tracing up the piercings along the underside. Opening my eyes I reached over and retrieved the lube that I had put there the night prior, pouring some into my hand to spread along my length. I wrapped my hand tightly around my cock, using the lube to make it slick. The wet sound of it as my hand slid along my cock only added to the soundtrack of Lexi's breathy voice as she begged through the speakers.

"I'm not sure that was good enough. Maybe you don't want this after all."

"Please, Sir. Please give me your cock."

A sense of satisfaction washed over me when I thought about her submissiveness to me in that bedroom. The control she allowed me to have over her.

"Color, baby girl."

"Green. God, so fucking green, Sir."

I should have spanked her ass for that response but I hadn't wanted to push her at the time.

I continued to squeeze and stroke my cock, my hips flexing involuntarily as I imagined the feel of my hand slapping hard against her beautiful ass cheek, watching the red blush of the burn rising to the surface of her skin before plunging my cock deep inside her tight pussy.

The sounds of her moans and whimpers grew louder through the speakers, almost as if she was beneath me once more.

"Wrap your legs around me."

I closed my eyes again, picturing her beautiful body writhing beneath me.

The video continued to play and I knew what it would show me even without looking at it. Lexi on the bed beneath me with her hands restrained to the head board as I pushed my cock deep inside her pussy. I heard our combined groans echo through the speaker and I tightened my fist further around my length, imagining the feel of her pussy clenching around my cock.

"God, you feel fucking incredible."

My hand moved faster, the wet sounds of lube and skin filling the room. I could feel the pressure building inside of me. The sensation of my hand moving up and down my length was electric, sending jolts of pleasure through me.

"Please, Sir."

"Don't you dare fucking cum."

Her whine echoed around the room as I recalled pulling out of her and turning her over. I heard the sound of my hand slapping against her ass cheek. Once. Twice.

Each moan that came through the speakers pushed me closer to the edge.

"Fuck, your ass looks so pretty in pink, baby girl."

Her whimpers made my cock throb in my hand as I lost myself in the pleasure of my own touch. The sounds she made as I plunged back inside her pussy in the video were fucking erotic. I could feel the pressure building, my balls tightening as I got closer and closer to the edge.

"Oh my god!"

I continued to stroke myself, imagining Lexi writhing beneath me, my hips nestled perfectly against her ass each time I buried myself inside her pussy. Over and over again. I could almost feel her tight, wet heat surrounding me. I could almost imagine breathy gasps and moans in my ear as I thrust into her.

"Please Sir, can I cum? Please?"

My hand moved harder and faster along my length, my other hand reaching down to squeeze my balls, my breaths coming out in ragged pants. The pressure was becoming almost unbearable and I knew I was on the edge.

"Cum for me, baby girl."

On cue, her scream sounded through the speakers, her cries and whimpers echoing around me. With a low growl I came hard, my hot cum spilling all over my hand as I continued to strangle out every last drop from my cock.

I collapsed back into the chair, panting heavily, riding out the waves of pleasure still pulsing through my system, basking in the afterglow of my own release.

Chapter 21

Alexis

Was I ready for what was to come? Well that was definitely a good question. Mentally, yes, I wasn't going to let that asshole Nick keep dictating my life. Physically, I was almost there, besides the occasional twinge of pain I felt almost completely back to normal. I was under orders from all the men in the house that I wasn't allowed to go back to exercising for a couple of weeks and even then I was to limit it to low impact exercises and to take it slowly.

Emotionally though, that was a completely different situation. I never thought I would allow myself to fall in love with someone after what I had gone through, let alone four someone's.

Looking around the kitchen at my men joking between themselves the next morning I could feel it tugging at my heart.

I knew that my feelings for each of them were different and unique, but it was still overwhelming to think about. I had always been independent and guarded with my emotions, but these men had managed to break down my walls and make me feel things I never thought I would feel again.

But with those emotions came fear. Fear that I would lose them, fear that they would hurt me, fear that I wasn't enough for them. I knew that I needed to talk to them about my fears and insecurities, but it was hard to open up and be vulnerable.

As I poured myself a cup of coffee and joined the conversation, I made a decision to take things one day at a time. To enjoy the moments we had together and not worry about what might happen in the future. To trust that they cared for me as much as I cared for them.

It wouldn't be easy, but I was determined to face my fears and allow myself to love and be loved.

"What is the plan for the day?" I asked looking towards Colt.

He rested his own coffee on the kitchen island and leaned over towards me. "Well, as we discussed, we need to go out and have a more public presence so Nick thinks he can get to you more easily."

I flicked my eyes towards Hunt and Gabe before hiding the slight blush that came to my face behind my coffee as I took a drink and remembered the public presence we made the day before.

Gabe grinned and opened his mouth to say something but Hunt interrupted him with a smack to the back of his head, obviously knowing what he was about to say. "Not that sort of presence," Hunt snarked at his brother.

Gabe shut his mouth but continued to grin as Colt and Rome looked between us all with raised brows.

Colt narrowed his eyes and frowned at them before returning his attention to me. "I thought I could give you a tour of the city, maybe take you out to lunch too."

I smiled at his thoughtfulness. "I'd really like that."

Hunt was also grinning now. "I'm happy to be your second escort if you would like." He threw me a wink.

Rome scoffed at him. "From the sounds of it you have socialized enough. I'll go."

I laughed and walked away, aiming for the room they allocated to me that I had yet to sleep in.

I sat down on the bed and took a deep breath, trying to calm my nerves. I knew that going out in public would be a big step for me, but I also knew that I couldn't let Nick control my life anymore. It was time for me to take back my power and live my life on my own terms.

With that thought in mind, I got up from the bed and started to get ready for the day ahead. I chose a simple outfit from the clothes we had bought: a red summer type dress that molded to my chest and waist before flaring slightly to fall loosely to my knees, and slipped on my new black sneakers.

As I walked back into the kitchen, the men turned to look at me, their eyes widening as they took in my appearance.

"Wow," Gabe said, grinning. "You look amazing."

Hunt whistled, while Rome and Colt simply smiled at me.

I felt a rush of confidence as I realized that I could do this. I could face the world with these men by my side and nothing could stop me.

With a smile on my face, I linked my arm with Colt's, and together we walked out of the house and into the bright sunlight with Rome following behind us, ready to take on whatever the day had in store for us.

After a short drive, Colt parked in a parking lot and we made our way into the bustle of the city. The sounds and smells overwhelmed me at first, but as we walked around, I began to relax and enjoy myself. We visited some of the city's famous landmarks and tourist spots, and I felt grateful to be experiencing it all with two of the men who had become so important to me.

As we walked, I could feel the eyes of people on us, but I refused to let it get to me. I kept my head held high and leaned into Colt's side for support. It felt good to have him there, to know that he was there to protect me if anything were to happen.

As we continued our walk around the city, taking in the sights and sounds of the busy streets, I felt a sense of freedom that I hadn't felt in a long time. For the first time in months, I felt like I was living my life instead of just surviving it.

It's late in the morning when Colt led me into a massive library. It's beautiful, and I found myself spinning in circles trying to take in all the arched ceilings and stained glass. I had never seen something so beautiful.

Colt chuckled and gently took my hand in his, leading me slowly through the rows and rows of books at a wandering pace, allowing me to take in everything. He looked at me out of the corner of his eyes but I still caught it since I was looking everywhere.

I grinned and ducked my head as he cleared his throat. "So, how was your shopping trip yesterday?" he asked.

My eyes widened slightly before I bit my lip. "It was good," I responded.

Colt chuckled. "Good huh? From what I was told I would have thought it was better than good." He glanced back at Rome who was walking closely behind us. "Remind me to tell the twins they need to up their game."

I laughed in astonishment. "No, they really don't," I clarified.

Colt hummed in response with a smile on his face. He stopped walking and tugged me into his body, his hand coming up to grip the back of my neck to draw my face towards his. "Well then, let's see if we can do better," he whispered to me before drawing my lips to his.

He pressed his body more firmly against mine as his mouth started to devour me, his other hand on my waist as he maneuvered us until my back was against something solid. I gasped into the kiss, Colt taking advantage to sweep his tongue into my mouth.

I moaned against him as my eyes fluttered closed, my hands gripped at his waist to try pulling him further into me.

His hand released the back of my neck to move around the front of my throat, his fingers squeezing my jaw and moving my face to the side as he kissed and nipped a path down my neck.

Blinking my eyes back open, I was startled by how close Rome was as he leaned against the stacks beside us. He was watching us with a fire in his eyes as he took in every little twitch of my body and pant of my breath.

There was no one near us and it took only a moment to realize Colt had slowly led us to the very back of the library and out of sight.

Colt brought my face back to his again, giving my jaw one last nip before moving so close to my face that his lips brushed mine as he spoke. "Do you have any idea what this dress has been doing to me since I first saw you in it?" His voice was a soft rasp.

I gave a slight shake of my head as I bit into my lip.

He moved the hand at my waist to grip my hand and moved it to his crotch. I felt his rock hard cock covered by his jeans.

I squeezed and we both moaned.

Colt's hand moved up to cover my mouth. "Let's try not to get caught, princess."

Chapter 22

Alexis

He took a step backwards, pulling me with him before turning me around to face the books. For a moment he didn't move and glancing back at him I saw his eyes narrowed as he looked at the books. He reached around me and plucked one from the shelf. He opened the book, flipping through the pages briefly before he placed it open on the shelf in front of us.

"Bend over princess, hands on the stacks," he said as his hand trailed softly down my back in encouragement.

I couldn't help the slight chuckle that escaped me but I did what I was told, bending over at the waist and placing my hands on the shelves in front of me until I was directly in line with the open book. Colt gripped my hips, moved me back, and used his hands to spread my legs. I felt him gather up the bottom of my dress and flip it up over my ass to rest bunched up on my back.

"We used up so much energy walking around this morning that I need a pre-lunch snack, princess. See that book in front of you? You're going to read that to me. And if you stop reading, well then I will stop eating," he said before he dropped to his knees behind me. His hands rubbed softly over the globes of my ass, gripping them with both hands before giving one a sharp slap that has me releasing a breathy moan. Moving his hands down and sliding his fingers beneath my underwear, he moved them aside and then I felt his breath against my pussy. I was strung tight with anticipation.

"Read, princess," he growled and I was startled into action.

I focused on the pages in front of me and quickly scanned the page as my eyes widened. Was he serious? This was not going to fucking help at all.

Clearing my throat I start to read softly. Colt chuckled and gave my other ass cheek a slap. "Loud enough for us to hear you princess," he said before sliding a finger through my wet pussy.

I choked on my breath and felt my face flush red. Glancing quickly at Rome from the corner of my eye, I saw him still leaning against the stacks watching everything with a smirk. I took a breath and started again, raising my voice a fraction. Hopefully enough for Colt to hear but not to carry to anyone else in the building.

"I was close to coming, but wasn't ready for it to end yet, so I pulled the vibrator away until I could calm down for a minute." Colt's tongue slid slowly up the length of my pussy, making my breath hitch, but I continued. "I returned it to its position and let it build up again. Just as I was getting close to coming, something made me open my eyes."

Colt's mouth started to move and slide against me a little more thoroughly, his tongue circling my clit before thrusting into my pussy.

"Dorian was standing in my doorway, basketball shorts, no shirt, both hands braced on either side of the doorjamb, staring at me with intense hunger in his eyes."

He sucked my clit into his mouth and my words faltered. He released it and moved away immediately. Fuck.

I forced myself to start again. "I sat up with a gasp, closing my legs and covering my bare breasts while I panted heavily. I was so close! If I squeezed my legs together, I would probably come."

Yeah I could totally appreciate where this woman was coming from.

Colt moved his mouth back to my pussy as I started again, swirling his tongue further around my clit before licking me from my clit to my ass.

"'Don't stop,' Dorian demanded, his voice low and gravelly. His hair was flat against his head as the rain continued to come down outside. 'Lean against the headboard and spread those legs.'"

Colt once again sucked my clit into his mouth and although my breath hitched I forced myself to continue.

"If I wasn't so desperate to come, I wouldn't have listened to him." Fuck yes, I wholeheartedly agreed. "Or so I told myself. I scooted back, so the headboard propped me up and spread my legs as he commanded."

I automatically shifted my legs further apart and pushed back with my hips, pushing my pussy towards Colt's face. He hummed approvingly and rewarded me by thrusting two fingers into my pussy as he flicked my clit with his tongue.

My voice was shaking as I pushed myself to keep reading. "'Turn towards me a little more so I can watch that wet pussy spasm when you come.'"

Oh. My. Fucking. God.

My pussy tightened around Colt's fingers as the combination of dirty talk in the book and Colt's movements pushed me right to the edge. "I didn't think I was one for dirty talking, but holy shit, he was getting me hot. I adjusted my body, so he had a clear view of my pussy." I read aloud, almost stumbling over the end of the sentence as Colt added another finger and thrust them hard and deep inside me, his tongue still swirling patterns around my clit.

"'Turn the setting down low and put it back on you.'" I whimpered as Colt slowed his movements, his tongue flicking against my clit in contrast to the slower pace of his fingers.

"I didn't need to ask what 'it' was. I turned down the intensity and put the vibrator back on my clit. I closed my eyes and leaned my head back."

Colt went back to thrusting his fingers into me harder, his tongue flicking and swirling around my clit with renewed vigor.

"'Open your eyes and look at me,' he said. I opened my eyes and glared at him."

My body was trembling, my pussy tightening around Colt's fingers as he curled them inside me to rub against my G-spot. The thumb of his other hand pressed against my rear entrance.

"H... he... chuck... chuckled." I stammered on a moan as Colt sucked my clit into his mouth again.

Rome leaned down close to my ear. "Good girl," he growled as I silently read the same line in the book and Colt brushed his teeth against me.

I was gone. Total sensory overload. My orgasm slammed into me, and I silently screamed into the hand Rome clamped around my mouth. My eyes rolled back as my pussy clamped down on Colt's fingers, pulsing in time with the waves of pleasure that washed over me.

As I started to come down from my orgasm Colt moved away, pulling his fingers from my pussy. I start to straighten only for a hand to press firmly on my back to keep me bent over.

"Don't move until you have permission." Rome growled, his hand sliding down to grip my ass cheek and dragging another whimper from me.

"I brought a present for you, baby girl," he said as I heard and felt him move to take Colt's place behind me on his knees. "I was going to give it to you at lunch but now seems like the perfect time."

He licked my pussy once and I shuddered at the stimulation, the sensation starting to drag me back towards another orgasm.

Then I felt something cold at my entrance moments before he was pushing it inside of me. My pussy clamped down on it automatically and I moaned again. He pushed hard on it until I felt the flared base of it press against me. The base seemed to be contoured and expanded so that it covered me all the way from my clit and over my entire pussy. Rome then moved my underwear back into place to cover whatever it was and then gently dragged my dress back down and over my ass, giving one cheek a soft squeeze.

He moved away again and there was silence for a moment as I grew accustomed to what he had pushed into my pussy.

"You can stand now, baby girl." Rome said finally and I stood back up. And moaned.

Whatever it was moved when I did.

I looked at him with wide eyes and a flushed face. He returned my look with intense eyes.

"You are to keep that in until I say so. And no cumming again without my permission. Understand, baby girl?" he said with a raised brow.

Well, fuck, this was going to be impossible.

I swallowed roughly before I nodded. "Yes, Sir," I breathed.

Chapter 23

Alexis

I was right. This was fucking impossible.

After we left the library we had taken a walk around a botanic garden, and I could have sworn they did it just for shits and giggles.

After stopping at least three times to get myself under control they finally took pity on me and ushered me into a beautiful restaurant within the gardens. The building was almost like a glass dome so that its patrons had an almost three hundred and sixty degree view of the surrounding nature. The kitchen itself was a sunken room in the center of the restaurant to allow for almost uninterrupted views. There were trees and plants interspersed throughout the tables to give each table some illusion of privacy and connection to the surrounding garden.

We were shown to a secluded spot towards the edge of the dome and I gratefully took a seat.

Only to regret it immediately when the chair only pushed against the flared base of the object in my pussy. My eyes closed on a shuddered breath.

I heard Colt chuckle, and I threw a glare his way which just made him laugh harder.

Rome's lip also twitched as he raised a brow at me. "How are you feeling, baby girl?"

I took a few deep breaths and straightened my spine, refusing to let him win. "I'm fine," I said through gritted teeth.

Rome chuckled at my response. "Really? That's good to hear."

Colt leaned forward, a devilish grin on his face. "You know, I think she needs a distraction."

Rome's eyes sparkled with amusement. "I think you might be right."

Rome reached into his pocket and pulled out a small black item. Before I could even register what it was he clicked a button on it.

Suddenly, the object in my pussy began to vibrate, sending shockwaves of pleasure through my entire body. I gasped and bit my lip to hold back a moan as my eyes widened in shock.

Colt leaned back with a satisfied smirk.

Rome raised an eyebrow as his lips twitched. "You okay, baby girl? You look a little flushed."

I nodded, unable to speak as the vibrations intensified suddenly. My body arched in response as I tried to control my breathing, my eyes closing involuntarily. I could feel myself propelling rapidly towards an orgasm, but just as I was about to tip over, the vibrations stopped.

I opened my eyes, panting, to see Colt and Rome exchanging a knowing look.

Colt leaned forward again and picked up the menu in front of him. "So, princess, what would you like to order for lunch?"

I gave him a withering look. "An orgasm," I snarked and he chuckled just as the waiter rounded a plant near our table and headed towards us.

The waiter arrived at our table and took our orders, seemingly unaware of the tension that was crackling in the air. Rome and Colt were both smirking, clearly enjoying the effect they were having on me. I tried to compose myself, taking deep breaths and trying to focus on something else, anything else, besides the throbbing sensation between my legs.

When the waiter left, Rome leaned forward and spoke in a low voice. "You're doing so well, baby girl. I'm proud of you."

I couldn't help but feel a sense of pride at his words. Despite the overwhelming sensations I was experiencing, I was managing to keep my composure.

The conversation turned to more mundane topics, and I tried my best to focus on the discussion at hand. But it was difficult, with the knowledge that Rome held the power to make me come undone at any moment.

As we ate our meal, I could feel the object inside me pressing against me with every movement. It was a constant reminder of my submission, and I couldn't deny the thrill it gave me.

As we finished eating, Rome leaned over to whisper in my ear. "You've been such a good girl, taking my little gift without complaint. I think you deserve a reward."

I felt a shiver run through my body at his words, and I looked up at him with wide eyes. "What kind of reward?" I asked hesitantly.

Rome leaned back in his chair, his lips curling into a wicked smile. "You'll see."

He reached into his pocket and pulled out the remote again, clicking a button on it. I felt the vibrations start up again, and I moaned softly, unable to control my response. Rome leaned forward and kissed me deeply, his tongue exploring my mouth as I writhed against the chair.

When he finally pulled away, I was panting and flushed, my body on fire. I was teetering on the edge of cumming, and then he switched it off again.

I whimpered.

Colt, the asshole, just signaled for the check and we left the restaurant. As we walked back to the car, I could feel the vibrations starting up again. I stumbled and bit my lip, trying to hold back a moan, but it was impossible. I could feel myself getting closer and closer to the edge again. I was so focused on not coming from the stimulation that I couldn't be bothered worrying if people around us even heard the noises I was making.

When we finally reached the car, Rome turned to me with a wicked grin. "Ready to go home, baby girl?"

I nodded, my breaths coming in short gasps. I was on the verge of coming undone, and I knew it wouldn't take much to push me over the edge.

The vibrations stopped again.

Fucking assholes.

As we drove back to the house, my pussy throbbed with need and desire, while the assholes in the front seat chatted quietly to themselves.

When we finally arrived at the house, Colt pulled me into his body again, kissing me deep and dirty before he turned me and pushed me in Rome's direction with a chuckle and a slap to my ass. Which just made my pussy clench around the toy, and I stumbled into Rome's arms.

Rome led me inside and up to his bedroom, locking the door with a loud click once we were inside.

I stood in the center of the room, unsure what to do. The anticipation of what was to come was almost too much to handle.

Rome walked over to me, his eyes dark with desire. He reached out and grabbed my hair, pulling my head back as he leaned in to kiss me deeply. I moaned against his lips, my body responding to his touch. He trailed his hand down my body, stopping just above my aching pussy.

"Did you enjoy your lunch, baby girl?" he whispered in my ear.

I nodded, unable to form words as the vibrations in my pussy suddenly started up again. My body trembled with pleasure as Rome's fingers danced over my sensitive skin.

"Good," he said, his voice low and husky as the vibrations stopped again. "Because dessert is about to be served. Take off your clothes," he commanded.

Without hesitation, I obeyed, stripping off my dress and bra, leaving me in just my panties. Rome circled around me, inspecting me from every angle.

"You're so beautiful," he murmured, before he stepped closer and ripped off my panties. I gasped at the suddenness of the action, but I was too turned on to care.

"What color are you at, baby girl?" he asked.

"Green, Sir." I responded breathlessly.

He hummed approvingly. "Are you sure you want this? We are in my space this time, I won't be holding back if you choose to play with me."

I nodded eagerly, my body aching for his touch. "Yes, Sir, please," I begged.

He hummed again and brushed his lips briefly at the corner of my mouth. "Kneel," he said softly. I immediately dropped to my knees, whimpering when the toy inside me moved again, anticipation buzzing through me. "From now on, if we are going to be playing, you are to be waiting on your knees on the floor in front of the bed, can you do that for me?"

I nodded and he gripped the hair at the top of my head.

"Remember to use your words," he reprimanded.

I moaned slightly at the tug on my hair. "Yes, Sir."

He released his grip and smoothed his hand down my hair. "Good girl," he praised before walking away towards the side of the room to a set of drawers there and started rifling through one of them.

"Is the wall currently a hard limit for you, baby girl?" he asked and I frowned in confusion.

He glanced at me and upon seeing my expression he indicated the blank wall next to him and the bolts installed on it that I hadn't noticed previously.

A cold shiver runs through me at the mental image. "Yes, Sir."

He simply nodded in response as though it was exactly what he expected as he started looking through the drawers.

I took a moment to take in the room. It was done in various shades of white, gray, and black and looked like a cross between a high tech office and a sleek and modern BDSM club. Along one wall was a high tech computer and monitor setup where I could tell he worked a lot.

Along the other wall was a different story. Now that he had pointed them out I could see various bolts and sliding bars installed on what I had taken for a blank wall. The bolts and bars then extended up onto the ceiling.

There was a tall set of sleek black drawers that Rome was pulling several items from. On the other side was another wall but that one was far from empty also, several items hung from hooks on that wall that just the sight of them made my pussy clench around the toy.

He had a large and varying selection of restraints, paddles, floggers and other items I wasn't able to readily identify. All were made of steel and black leather.

Fuck. Me.

Seriously, rest in peace to my pussy. That wall was hot.

He then carried the items he collected over to the bedside table before he moved around to sit on the end of the bed facing towards me.

He raised a brow at me. "You're meant to be over here, baby girl," he said, indicating to the floor in front of him, a good three meters away from where I currently knelt.

I went to stand to move over to him but he stopped me with a look and a gesture. "No. Since you're on your knees in the wrong place, you stay on them until you're in the right place. Crawl to me."

Chapter 24

Alexis

My eyes widened at the command, but I obeyed, moving to my hands and knees and starting to crawl to him. Only to freeze the moment the toy shifted inside me yet again.

I saw the twitch of his lips that indicated he knew exactly what he was doing to me with the command, and I was proven correct when he grabbed the remote from his pocket and turned it back on.

Fuck. Me.

I moaned and almost came on the spot, barely controlling myself as I hung my head, and breathed deeply to center myself.

"That wasn't a request. Surely you're not disobeying me already," Rome said. It made me want to be an absolute brat, but I was desperate to cum, and I knew if I did act out he would deny me even longer.

I pushed myself forward, moving slowly as I crawled across the floor to him. I was panting and trembling by the time

I rested on my ankles at his feet, whimpering as the move pushed the vibrations more firmly against my clit.

I was so fucking close to not being able to hold off my orgasm any longer when he switched off the toy again. I almost sighed in relief.

He brushed strands of hair off my face before smoothing a hand over my head again. "You're such a good girl for me. You're doing so well."

My pussy throbbed at the praise and I whimpered with need.

"Color, baby girl?" He asked softly.

"Green, Sir." I replied with a trembling voice.

He stood up from the bed still looking down at me. "Take my clothes off." He commanded.

I reached out and slowly and methodically got to work removing his clothes, starting with his pants. I almost drooled when his hard cock was released from its confines almost directly in my face, the metal piercings along the underside glinting from the light. I wanted so desperately to lean forward and run my tongue along those piercings and return even a tiny amount of the torture I was feeling.

Instead I forced myself to my feet to remove his shirt, letting my fingers drag slowly against his skin as I raised it up his chest and over his head. There was humor on his face as he slid his hands into my hair on both sides of my face and leant down to take my mouth in a deep slow kiss.

He pulled away and gestured to the bed. "Lie down," he said.

I did as I was told, my heart racing with anticipation as I laid on my back in the center of the bed. He crawled onto the bed and straddled me, his hands running up and down my body. He leaned down and kissed me softly, his lips barely brushing against mine.

"Are you ready for your reward, baby girl?" he whispered.

I nodded, my breaths coming in short gasps. I was ready for anything he had in store for me.

"Use your words, baby girl," he said.

"Yes, Sir," I moaned.

He reached over to where he had put the remote. He clicked a button on it, and I felt the vibrations start up again, stronger than ever before.

I moaned, my body arching off the bed. He held me down, his fingers teasing at my nipples as the vibrations pushed me closer and closer to the edge.

"Cum for me, baby girl," he said in a low voice. "I want to see you come undone."

And then he turned it up a notch, and I came apart with a scream, my body shaking with pleasure, my fingers clawing at the sheets.

The orgasm seemed to go on forever, waves of ecstasy tearing through me.

He clicked the remote off, and I collapsed back onto the bed, panting hard.

Rome leaned down and kissed me softly, his hands gentle as they stroked my skin.

"Good girl," he whispered against my lips.

He kissed me deeply, his hands sliding over my body and I moaned into his mouth, completely lost in the sensations.

He broke the kiss, his lips trailing down my neck, nipping and sucking at my skin. I arched my back, my hands gripping his shoulders as he continued his assault on my body. He made his way down my body, kissing and licking his way to my breasts, taking one of my nipples into his mouth and sucking hard.

I cried out, my fingers tangling in his hair, urging him on. He switched to my other breast, giving it the same attention before moving lower, his tongue circling my navel before finally reaching my throbbing clit.

He hovered over me, his eyes intense as he reached down and slowly pulled the toy out of me.

I gasped as he tossed it aside and lowered his head to my pussy, sucking on my clit and licking up my release. I writhed beneath him, my hands clutching at the sheets as he brought me closer and closer to another orgasm.

He licked and sucked, alternating between gentle flicks of his tongue and harder sucks on my clit, sending me barrelling towards the edge. I moaned loudly, my body arching off the bed as he expertly worked his tongue on and in me.

Just as I was about to cum again, he stopped, leaving me panting and desperate.

I whimpered in frustration, my body on fire with need. Rome looked up at me with a wicked grin, his eyes dark with desire. "Not yet, baby girl," he said. "We're just getting started."

And with that, he continued his relentless assault on my body, bringing me to the edge time and time again before pulling back. Finally after what felt like an eternity he thrust his fingers into my aching pussy setting a slow rhythm as he licked and sucked my clit, stopping just as I was about to cum. He reached over to the items he had pulled from the drawer and moments later a buzzing sound filled the air as he raised his head away from my pussy, looking along my shaking body at my sweat and tear covered face. "Cum again for me, baby girl," he rasped before he held the vibrating toy directly against my clit and curled his fingers inside me.

I screamed as my body exploded with pleasure, my orgasm crashing over me like a tidal wave. Rome continued to work me through my release, his fingers never faltering as he drew out every last tremble and shudder from my body.

He finally slowed his movements, pulling his fingers from me and turning off the vibrator. He kissed his way up my limp body, his lips leaving a trail of fire in their wake. He hovered over me, his eyes dark with desire.

As I came down from my high, he leaned over closer, his lips brushing against my ear. "You're so beautiful when you cum, baby girl," he whispered.

I whimpered, feeling my body still thrumming with pleasure. "Thank you, Sir," I gasped out, my voice barely above a whisper.

He chuckled, the sound rumbling through his chest. "Thanking me for what, baby girl?" he asked, his lips trailing down my neck.

"For...for making me cum, Sir," I managed to get out, my breath still coming in short gasps.

"That's right," he said, his hand sliding down to cup my pussy, feeling the wetness still coating my skin. "That's because you're ours," he growled. "You belong to us and no one else."

I shivered at his possessive tone, my body responding to his dominance. "Yes, I'm yours," I moaned, my hands moving to grip his hair.

He lifted his head, his eyes burning with lust. "Say it again," he demanded.

"I'm yours," I gasped out, my body arching towards him.

"You came because I wanted you to, because I knew just how to make you feel good."

I moaned, my body arching into his touch. "Yes, Sir," I said, my voice still barely a whisper.

"Good girl," he said, his fingers sliding inside me again, setting a slow rhythm that had me moaning. "Right now you're mine to play with, mine to pleasure and I'm going to make sure you feel so good."

I whimpered, feeling a fresh wave of desire wash over me at his words. "Yes, Sir," I said, my body already starting to respond to his touch.

Chapter 25

Alexis

His eyes were burning as he looked down at me. "Color, baby girl?"

"So green, Sir." I whimpered and trembled at his touch.

He withdrew his fingers from my pussy again. I almost growled before he completely sat up and away from my body. His eyes raked over my naked and panting body for a moment before he reached out and rolled me over onto my stomach. He lifted my ass by my hips and pulled them towards him, dragging my upper body along the bed until my body was in a position that reminded me of a modified downward facing dog.

I yelped in shock as he bit the flesh of one of my ass cheeks, and then he slapped the place he had just bitten. Heat shot through me and straight to my pussy making me moan.

His fingers soothed over the burn with a low chuckle.

He used his other hand to move my legs apart.

Once my legs were in the exact position he wanted, he brushed a thumb against my rear entrance. "Can I play here, baby girl?" he asked softly, his thumb gradually pressing down firmly.

"Yes, Sir." I moaned into the mattress.

He removed his thumb and I heard rustling before his fingers returned wet with what I assumed was lube. He pushed slowly inside with one finger.

I gasped at the sensation, feeling the mix of pleasure and discomfort. Rome continued to push his finger inside, slowly working it in and out to stretch me. I focused on relaxing and breathing deeply, trying to get used to the sensation.

"Good girl," Rome murmured, his voice low and soothing. "Relax for me."

I nodded, my eyes closed as I concentrated on letting go of the tension in my body. Rome added a second finger, and I gasped at the sensation of being stretched even further. He moved his fingers in and out, scissoring them to open me up, giving me time to relax and get used to the sensation.

I moaned softly as he added a third finger, feeling the fullness of his hand inside me. His other hand then slid up my back, tracing circles along my skin and sending shivers down my spine.

After a few more moments of exploration, he withdrew his fingers and I heard him apply more lube. But it wasn't his cock or his fingers I felt being pushed inside me next.

Instead, I felt the cool, smooth surface of a butt plug being pressed against my entrance. Rome worked it in slowly, letting me adjust to the size and shape of it. The plug filled me up, making me feel stretched and full in a way that was both overwhelming and exciting. I gasped at the sudden fullness, feeling the plug stretch me out even more than his fingers had.

My body responded eagerly, arching up towards him.

"Good girl," Rome murmured, his hand stroking my back again. "You're doing so well."

I moaned in response, the sensation of being filled and his praise driving me wild. Rome continued to move the plug in and out, gradually increasing the speed and intensity. The pleasure was overwhelming, building and building until I couldn't take it anymore.

"That's it, baby girl," Rome rasped. "You take it so well. Such a good girl for me."

"Please, Sir," I begged, my body trembling with need. "Please let me cum."

Rome chuckled darkly. "Not yet, baby girl," he said, his voice full of desire. "I want to feel you cum around my cock."

I whimpered at his words, feeling the heat and desire building inside me.

He pushed the plug deep inside of me again and then left it there.

I heard the cap of the lube open again moments before I felt his cock at my pussy.

"Color, baby girl?" He asked as he paused.

"Fuck, green, give me your cock," I demanded in frustration.

He slapped my ass cheek hard and I cried out, the ripple effect moving like fire everywhere in my already overheated body. My body tightened around the plug seconds before he started pushing his cock into my pussy.

I gasped at the sensation, feeling a mix of pleasure and pain as he filled me up slowly, pushing me beyond anything

I had ever felt before. I felt every barbell piercing along the underside of him as each of them entered me until he was filling me up completely.

The sensation of being so stretched to my limits was almost too much. The feeling riding that thin line of both too much and not enough. The thought of saying yellow briefly flashed across my mind as he paused for a moment, allowing me to adjust. Then he started to move slowly in and out. He kept his movements gentle and controlled, guiding me with his hands. As he moved inside me, the piercings scraped against my sensitive walls and I felt a new level of pleasure building within me. A sense of fullness that I had never experienced before was consuming me. It was so tight I felt everything as he moved.

I moaned loudly as he thrust deeper and harder, my body writhing beneath him. He leaned down and whispered in my ear, his breath hot against my skin. "You feel so fucking good, baby girl, so tight and hot and wet." he said. "I love watching you take my cock like a good girl."

With those words, I felt a new level of desire and pleasure surge through me, and I pushed back against him, taking him deeper inside me. He responded with a low groan of pleasure and increased his pace, his hands gripping my hips hard as he thrust into me more forcefully. I felt my body responding, my muscles clenching around him and building towards another orgasm.

"That's it, baby girl," Rome groaned. "Strangle my cock with this perfect pussy, take me deep inside you."

He released one of my hips and pressed hard against the plug in my ass and suddenly it started vibrating. My pussy tightened painfully hard around him and his pace faltered.

"Cum for me, baby girl, scream my fucking name."

And then it hit me, like a tidal wave of pleasure crashing over me. And yes I screamed his name as I came, my body shaking with the intensity of it. Rome slammed his cock into me hard and I felt him cum deep inside me, his own orgasm tearing through him with a low groan that I felt through my entire body.

As the waves of pleasure slowly subsided, Rome collapsed onto me, his weight heavy and comforting. We lay there for a few moments, catching our breaths, before he slowly withdrew from me. The plug was still inside me, vibrating gently, and I shuddered as it continued to stimulate me.

Rome reached down and gently removed the plug, his fingers trailing over my sensitive skin. "You did so well, baby girl," he said softly, pressing a gentle kiss to the back of my neck. "I'm so proud of you."

I smiled contentedly, feeling a warm glow spreading through my body. "Thank you, Sir," I murmured.

I heard him move away for a moment before he returned, wiping me completely clean with warm washcloths before rolling me onto my back and doing the same to the front of my body. He then took the toys and clothes to the bathroom and I heard him clean everything.

When he returned to bed after a brief detour to his computer, he wrapped his arms around me and pulled me close. We drifted off to sleep, wrapped in each other's arms.

Chapter 26

Gabe

I was just getting ready for bed when I heard it.

At first, I didn't know what I was hearing, but mere seconds later I couldn't believe what I had just heard.

Lexi.

I heard her gasp echo through the air and for a moment panic started to take over before I recognized that it came from our internal speaker system. It didn't take long to realize what I was hearing when I heard what came next.

"What color are you at, baby girl?"

"Green, Sir."

That asshole.

He was playing the sound of them together through the whole house.

I heard Rome hum. *"Are you sure you want this? We are in my space this time, I won't be holding back if you choose to play with me."*

"Yes, Sir, please."

I could hear the need in her voice even through the speakers.

Walking to the door in just my pants I opened it to look out into the hallway and saw Hunt leaning against his own door frame frowning in the direction of Rome's room.

"Kneel."

I choked on my own breath and braced my hand against my door frame.

"From now on, if we are going to be playing, you are to be waiting on your knees on the floor in front of the bed, can you do that for me?... Remember to use your words."

My wide eyes met Hunt's as we heard her moan in response. *"Yes, Sir."*

"Good girl."

I saw Colt move into our line of vision from his doorway as he pointed a firm finger at each of us, a slight smile tugging at the corner of his mouth. "Not a word to her about this."

"Is the wall currently a hard limit for you, baby girl?"

"Yes, Sir."

Colt's breath caught and he frowned slightly as he flicked a glance at Rome's door, a sad look flashing across his face. I frowned at him, knowing exactly where his mind went at that moment. I thought it best to bring him back on topic.

"Did you know he was going to do this?" I asked him.

He gave me a smirk. "We may have been playing a little earlier, and I might have said something about having a quiet night without being able to hear her."

"You're meant to be over here, baby girl.... No. Since you're on your knees in the wrong place, you stay on them until you're in the right place. Crawl to me."

We heard movement through the speakers before a loud moan sounded.

Colt tilted his head as he looked up thoughtfully, as though he were listening more intently. "He must have left the toy in her pussy."

"Fuck," I mumbled and spun on my heels, quickly returning to my room as I heard Colt chuckle behind me. Closing the door I leaned against it and closed my eyes, breathing deeply to try and slow my heart rate.

"That wasn't a request. Surely you're not disobeying me already."

I heard movement and then I heard her whimper. The sounds were making me rock fucking hard.

"You're such a good girl for me. You're doing so well."

I heard her whimper yet again and I groaned, rubbing the heel of my palm hard against my rigid cock before gripping it through my pants. She was such a good girl for us it turned me on just picturing her on her knees like I knew she would be.

"Color, baby girl?"

"Green, Sir."

"Take my clothes off."

I groaned again and shoved my own pants down and off my legs, stepping out of them as I made my way over to sit on the side of my bed and wrap my hand around my cock. I was certain Colt and Hunt would be doing exactly the same thing given the circumstance, listening to Lexi's moans and whimpers made it inevitable.

"Lie down."

I retrieved the lube from my side table, pouring some into my hand before I shifted on the bed and leaned back against the headboard to get more comfortable. I wrapped my lube covered hand around my cock again and slid it along the entire sensitive length, coating it and making it slick and wet.

"Are you ready for your reward, baby girl?" I heard almost inaudible gasps of breath before Rome said, *"Use your words, baby girl."*

I heard her moan, *"Yes, Sir."*

I could now hear the telltale buzz of a toy and she let out a deep moan. The sound pulled a soft groan from me as I squeezed my cock again, brushing a thumb over the piercing in the head.

"Cum for me, baby girl, I want to see you come undone."

I heard the buzzing get louder before her scream echoed through the house. I closed my eyes, laying fully on the bed as I squeezed the end of my cock. Something told me this was just the start.

"Good girl."

I started stroking my cock slowly, my hand moving up and down as I imagined I was pushing it in and out of Lexi's beautiful mouth. The whimpers and moans playing through the speakers went perfectly with the scene playing out in my mind and made it surreal. Picturing her pretty hazel eyes looking up at me with hunger while I wrapped a hand around her long brown hair and used it as an anchor to push deeper until I felt her swallow around me.

Fuck. I squeezed hard as I heard her whimper loudly again.

"Not yet, baby girl... We're just getting started."

I slowed down my movements again, my breathing heavy as I listened. I didn't want this to be over quickly either. And even though I knew that it wasn't me giving her this pleasure, I couldn't help but feel a sense of pride knowing that it was one of us making her feel so good.

"Cum again for me, baby girl."

Her scream echoed through the speakers again. I let out a low growl, feeling the tightness in my groin intensify as I listened to Lexi's second orgasm.

"You're so beautiful when you cum, baby girl."

As I listened to Lexi's sounds of pleasure, I found myself getting more and more turned on. My hand moved faster along my cock, and I let out a low groan.

"Thank you, Sir."

"Thanking me for what, baby girl?"

"For...for making me cum, Sir."

I took the opportunity to slow down my hand again and savor the moment. I wanted to enjoy the pleasure and make it last as long as possible.

"That's right... That's because you're ours... You belong to us and no one else."

"Yes, I'm yours."

"Say it again."

"I'm yours."

Fuck that did something to me. The possessive animal in my soul enjoyed hearing Lexi say those words. I looked forward to making her repeat them over and over again, hopefully with my cock buried deep inside her.

"You came because I wanted you to because I knew just how to make you feel good."

"Yes, Sir."

"Good girl...Right now you're mine to play with, mine to pleasure and I'm going to make sure you feel so good."

"Yes, Sir."

The combination of Lexi's moans and Rome's commands was almost too much to handle. I wanted to hear more, to feel more, to be a part of this experience for as long as possible.

"Color, baby girl?"

"So green, Sir."

The sound of her pleasure was like music to my ears, and it only served to heighten my own arousal. I could feel my body tensing as I approached the edge of my own orgasm, but I held back, wanting to savor the moment.

"Can I play here, baby girl?"

"Yes, Sir."

I felt my own release building, my hand moving faster and faster over my hard cock. The sounds of pleasure coming from the speakers were too much to resist. I was lost in the moment, completely caught up in the sexual energy of the scene playing out over the speakers.

"Good girl."

I couldn't help but picture a toy being pushed slowly into her ass. I groaned softly as I imagined her on all fours, the plug stretching her tight little hole as she waited for us to use her.

"Relax for me."

The sounds continued through the speakers, each moan and whimper fueling my own arousal. My cock twitched at the thought of my cock buried deep in her ass instead of the toy.

"Good girl."

But I didn't want to cum yet. I wanted to be in the moment with them, to imagine every detail of what was happening to Lexi as she moaned and writhed in pleasure.

"You're doing so well."

It was intense, and I could feel my body responding to the erotic audio. I focused on the sensation of my hand moving up and down my cock, the slickness of the lube, and the heat building up inside me.

"That's it, baby girl."

The sound of her breathing was ragged and heavy, punctuated by the occasional moan or whimper. I could tell that she was close to the edge again, and I felt a surge of excitement at the thought of her coming undone once more.

"You take it so well. Such a good girl for me."

I picked up the pace of my hand, my own breathing becoming ragged as I felt my orgasm building. The sounds from the speakers were driving me wild, fueling my desire and pushing me closer and closer to the edge.

"Please, Sir."

I could hear her gasping for breath, and I knew she was close to the edge again.

"Please let me cum."

The moans and whimpers coming from Lexi were becoming more urgent, more desperate.

"Not yet, baby girl."

I could feel the tension building in my body, my muscles tightening and my breath becoming more ragged.

"I want to feel you cum around my cock."

It was almost too much for me to handle, and I found myself speeding up my movements again, unable to resist the urge to bring myself to the brink.

"Color, baby girl?"

"Fuck, green, give me your cock."

It was clear that she was enjoying every moment of it, and the thought of her being used in such a way only made my own arousal burn hotter. I could feel my own need building, and I knew I wouldn't be able to hold back for much longer.

"You feel so fucking good, baby girl, so tight and hot and wet."

The sounds of pleasure continued through the speakers, growing louder and more intense with each passing moment. I could feel myself getting closer to losing control, the pressure in my cock building with each stroke. I could only imagine how she must be feeling, completely lost in the pleasure of the moment.

"I love watching you take my cock like this."

The sounds continued, the moans and whimpers growing louder and more desperate. I could hear the rustling of sheets and the creaking of the bed as they moved and shifted, lost to the sensations of the moment.

"That's it, baby girl... Strangle my cock with this perfect pussy, take me deep inside you."

I could hear the wet sounds of skin slapping against skin, mixed with Lexi's moans and the buzzing of a toy. I couldn't resist any longer, and I started stroking my cock harder and faster, imagining that it was me pounding into Lexi's tight little pussy.

"Cum for me, baby girl, scream my fucking name."

The sound of her moans turned into a scream as she reached her peak, the sound echoing through the speakers and sending me over the edge as well. My orgasm ripped through me, making me see stars as I spilled over my hand, my body shaking with pleasure as I rode out the orgasm.

"You did so well, baby girl... I'm so proud of you."

"Thank you, Sir."

I lay there for a few moments, catching my breath and letting my heart rate slow down. Then, with a deep sigh, I got up and headed for the shower.

Chapter 27

Alexis

Over the next few days, our routine settled back in, albeit with a significant difference. I found myself spending a lot of time in public places, no longer confined to the house, yet always with at least two of the men with me as my constant companions. Despite the new routine, there was an odd sense of normalcy to it all, with one glaring exception: I was forbidden from exercising until I saw the doctor again. It was driving me crazy. I had always used physical activity as a way to clear my head and stay centered, and without it, I felt adrift.

I even contemplated resorting to violence if I didn't get my way soon.

Today was the day of my appointment, and Gabe and Hunt were accompanying me to a private doctor's office. Apparently, they had connections with this particular physician and had already informed her about what I had been through. I wasn't sure what to expect, but I definitely wasn't prepared for the pristine, modern space that greeted me. The walls were painted in soothing shades of white and beige, and the receptionist offered a friendly smile as she checked me in. A nurse led me to a room to draw blood and collect a urine sample, and explained that they needed to test for any infections or complications arising from my injuries. After she finished, she sent me back out to the waiting room to wait for the doctor.

Gabe and Hunt flanked me in the plush waiting room, their concern and support palpable. I was grateful for their presence; it helped alleviate some of the nervousness that had crept up inside me. Finally, the door to the exam room opened, and Dr. Reynolds, a middle-aged woman with a warm smile, greeted me and ushered me inside. I took a deep breath, feeling reassured by the guys' supportive energy, even though they stayed behind in the waiting room.

"Good morning," Dr. Reynolds said with a professional smile. "I'm Dr. Reynolds. It's good to see you up and about after what you've been through."

Dr. Reynolds sat across from me and began examining the stitches on my ribs. It was uncomfortable, and I winced as she prodded the tender skin, but she assured me that everything was healing well. Suddenly, her next words shook me to my core.

"Looks like you're healing nicely," she said, her fingers deftly probing my skin. "I checked all your test results, and there are no infections or complications that could risk the baby, which is a relief."

My heart stopped at her words. What baby? I was on birth control injections. Wasn't I? Panic rose in my chest, and I struggled to maintain my composure. My mind went blank; I couldn't be pregnant. I had been so careful with my birth control. But had I missed one during my escape to the safe house?

Dr. Reynolds didn't seem to notice my shock. "Don't worry," she said. "The injuries you sustained and the stress of the abduction haven't affected the baby. You'll need to start taking prenatal vitamins and come back for regular check-ups, but otherwise, everything should be fine."

I nodded absently, barely registering her words.

Dr. Reynolds continued on, oblivious to the inner turmoil I was feeling. "Do you know roughly when you conceived? We can get your first follow up appointments set up."

Umm, how the fuck did she expect me to think right now.

I tried to work it out in my head. "I think about nineteen days ago," I rasped.

Dr. Reynolds jotted down the information, her expression still professional and calm. "Alright, we'll calculate your estimated due date based on the information you have given us which should put you at roughly 3 weeks pregnant, which correlates with your lab results. We'll go ahead and schedule your first follow-up appointment for next week. In the meantime, make sure to take the prenatal vitamins as prescribed, and try to take it easy and avoid any strenuous activities."

Her words echoed in my mind as I struggled to process the situation. I was pregnant. The realization hit me like a tidal wave, crashing over me with a mix of emotions. Fear, confusion, and disbelief swirled within me. How could this have happened? I thought I had taken all the necessary precautions.

Dr. Reynolds seemed to sense my distress and leaned forward, her voice gentle. "I understand that this might be overwhelming for you right now. It's normal to feel a range of emotions. If you have any questions or concerns, I'm here to support you."

I mustered the strength to speak, my voice trembling. "But I was on birth control injections. How is this possible?"

Dr. Reynolds nodded understandingly. "Birth control methods, including injections, can be highly effective, but they are not 100% foolproof. There is still a small margin of error. It's possible that a missed or delayed injection, or a variation in your hormone levels, could have contributed to this."

My mind was racing, trying to comprehend what this meant for me and my future. Gabe and Hunt were waiting for me in the waiting room, and I couldn't bring myself to tell them yet. I needed some time to process this on my own.

As we left the doctor's office and stepped out into the bright sunlight, I took a deep breath and tried to focus on the present moment, feeling the warmth of the sun on my skin and the cool breeze on my face.

Gabe and Hunt immediately noticed something was wrong, exchanging concerned glances. They asked if everything was alright, but I brushed off their concerns, telling them that I was just tired from the doctor's visit. I knew I couldn't keep this secret forever, but I needed more time to come to terms with the news.

My mind was in a fog. How could I have been so careless? And what was I going to do now? I had always wanted children someday, but not while I was still being hunted by a madman.

The ride back to the house was quiet, the only sound was the hum of the engine and the occasional rustle of fabric as one of the men shifted in their seat. I closed my eyes and tried to focus on my breathing, attempting to calm the racing thoughts in my mind.

As we arrived at the house, they asked me if I wanted to watch a movie with them.

"I just need a moment alone," I managed to say, my voice barely above a whisper. Gabe and Hunt exchanged another glance, silently acknowledging my request, and gave me a reassuring nod before heading to the kitchen.

I made my way to my room, closing the door behind me and sinking onto the bed. The reality of the situation was starting to sink in, and I felt a mix of fear and excitement wash over me. I'm going to be a mother, and my life was about to change in ways I couldn't even imagine.

I'm not sure how long I sat there staring off into space when my door opened and Rome slipped into the room, closing the door behind him. I smiled at him as he made his way over to stand in front of me.

I looked up at him from where I sat, his height so pronounced from my position and he reinforced that as he brushed a hand over my hair and then cradled the back of my head as he leaned over to brush his lips against mine.

He leaned back again but still stayed within my space. "Did you forget who I am? Did you think I wouldn't access your medical records from today to make sure you were okay?"

I felt a mix of relief and annoyance at his words. Of course, he had checked my medical records; he was always one step ahead, even when I didn't want him to be.

"I didn't forget who you are," I replied, my voice soft. "I just needed some time to process everything before telling anyone."

Rome nodded, his expression serious. "I understand, and I won't tell anyone. But you know we're all here for you, right? Whatever you need, we'll make sure you have it."

I nodded, feeling grateful for his support. "Thank you, Rome. I appreciate it."

He leaned down and kissed me again, his lips warm and reassuring. "We'll get through this together," he murmured against my lips.

I felt a surge of love and gratitude towards him and the other men, knowing that I could count on them no matter what. As I leaned into his embrace, I knew that everything would be okay, even if it was not exactly what I had planned for my life.

Suddenly, Hunt barged into the room and for a moment my heart was in my throat thinking somehow he knew now too.

"We have an emergency job, but we can't leave you here unprotected so you're coming with us," he said in a rush.

"What?" I responded in shock, looking between Rome and Hunt.

Rome closed his eyes, rubbing at the bridge of his nose at this sudden development.

"Hurry up and grab your gun sweetheart, your chariot awaits." Hunt grinned, completely oblivious to what was going on.

Rome looked at him seriously. "We will meet you down-stairs," he said, effectively dismissing Hunt, who frowned and left the room.

Rome looked back towards me. "I know I said I wouldn't tell anyone but when it comes to Colt, you need to tell him. If you don't then those medical records will make it to his desk."

My mouth dropped open in shock. "You would do that?" I asked.

His face softened. "Baby girl, he needs to know what he needs to protect."

Chapter 28

Alexis

Rome helped me strap on a vest and extra weapons before we both went downstairs to meet the others and pile into the vehicle.

Colt gave us a rundown while we were on our way. Apparently there had been intel that came in that showed a high ranking member of a terrorist organization was seen close by and there were no other teams available locally that could move on such short notice. Rome brought up details for the target on a tablet and passed it around to us to become familiar with who we needed to find. We were to locate and secure him for the government agents who were also on the way but weren't as close as us.

We approached the location slowly, taking in the suburban location. There were homes lined in a row and for a moment I felt like I had entered the land of the stepford wives when I saw all the similar cars parked in driveways. It seemed odd that a terrorist member would be hiding out in smallville but I guess it helped him keep a low profile.

Colt parked the vehicle a distance away behind a bunch of trees before we all stepped out and gathered out of sight. Going over the information we had on the location we formulated a plan of the best way to approach. I was to stay with Rome and Colt while the twins were to approach from the other direction after moving the car to that side.

We made our way towards the house, taking care to remain hidden from any potential threats. As we got closer, we could see that the house was a large, two-story building with a well-manicured lawn and a white picket fence surrounding it.

Colt signaled through earpieces for us to split up, with the twins taking the back entrance while we approached from the front. Rome and I followed Colt, who had already started to pick the lock on the front door.

Once inside, we could hear movement coming from upstairs. We quickly made our way up the stairs, our weapons drawn and ready for any surprises. As we approached the top of the stairs, we could hear voices coming from one of the rooms.

Colt signaled for us to take positions outside the door while he opened it quietly. As he pushed the door open, we saw a man sitting at a desk, typing on a laptop. He seemed surprised to see us, but before he could react, Colt had his weapon aimed at him.

"Freeze," Colt said in a stern voice. "You're under arrest for your involvement in terrorist activities."

The man tried to reach for a gun under his desk, but Colt was too quick for him. He tackled the man to the ground, disarming him in the process.

Colt was dragging the man back up when all hell broke loose.

A group of men stormed the room through another doorway with weapons aimed directly at us before opening fire. We took cover quickly and returned fire.

The man we were sent to capture though, wasn't quick enough, taking a bullet straight through his forehead and slumping to the ground, dead.

"Fuck, who are these guys." Colt growled.

I scoffed at him. "Obviously not the good guys."

Rome tried to drag me behind him but I shrugged him off and sent a glare his way only to receive a growl in response.

We weren't getting anywhere crouched where we were, and I could see that the twins were in much the same position in the doorway we had entered from.

After a few minutes the sound of gunshots slowed to a stop and when I chanced a peek over the desk there was a man looking directly at me with a brow raised. He chuckled.

"You know, there's really no need for everyone to die today. We just need the girl and then we can be on our way," he said, still laughing.

Fuck. Seriously? How the hell did they even know I was going to be there?

I gritted my teeth, tightening my grip on my weapon. These mercenaries were obviously not here for the same reasons we were. They must have been hired by Dominick to get to me.

I quickly scanned the room, looking for any potential exits or ways to gain the upper hand.

I glanced over at Colt, who was checking his weapon and giving us a nod. We knew what we had to do.

With a signal from Colt, we all sprang into action. Rome and I provided cover fire while Colt and the twins moved to flank the mercenaries. It was chaos, but we managed to take out the mercenaries quickly and gain the upper hand.

In the end, only the man who spoke remained. He held his hands up in surrender; he was no longer laughing when we took his weapons away.

"Did Dominick send you?" I demanded, pressing the barrel of my weapon to his forehead.

He chuckled again, his eyes glinting with amusement, obviously deciding he didn't care if he died. "Does it really matter? You were just a job, little girl."

I pressed the barrel harder against his skin, my anger and frustration boiling over. "How the fuck did you know where I was?"

"Lexi." Rome growled behind me before he tugged me backwards and away from the man. I shrugged him off again but stayed back.

"So Dominick sent you to retrieve me?" I snarled, wishing I could just shoot him.

He chuckled again. "Apparently he doesn't take kindly to people taking what's his. He wants them dead too," he said, motioning to the guys.

"Well you can pass on a message to your master. If he wants me, he can come get me himself." With that I raised my gun and shot him in the shoulder. I wanted him to deliver the message after all.

We left the man screaming and crying on the floor of the house as we made our way back to our vehicle in silence.

I could feel my adrenaline starting to dissipate, replaced by a feeling of unease. The fact that Dominick had hired mercenaries to come after me meant that he was getting desperate. It was only a matter of time before he came after me himself.

Colt started up the vehicle and we all climbed in, each of us silent as we processed what had just happened. Rome sat in the front, his eyes fixed on the road ahead as he made a call. I could tell he was angry, but he kept his thoughts to himself.

It wasn't until we were on the highway and out of danger that Colt finally broke the silence. "You did good, princess," he said, his eyes watching me in the mirror.

I nodded, not trusting myself to speak. The events of the last few hours had left me feeling drained, emotionally and physically. Hunt reached over and took my hand, giving it a gentle squeeze.

When Rome got off the phone from updating the agents he stared stoically out the window. The tension was palpable and I could feel the others looking between us as we made our way home.

Once we had arrived home we all made our way into the house. My intentions to go straight back up to my room were halted as Rome called my name. I spun around to find him standing close behind me, and I shoved him in the chest. Which had no effect on him.

I saw Gabe and Hunt retreat towards the kitchen out of the corner of my eye.

"Don't ever do that to me again." I snarled at him, pointing my finger in his face. I knew I must look like a petulant child.

He just growled in response, stepping forward to get in my face. "You know exactly why I did it."

Colt stepped between us, looking surprised by the turn of events. "What the fuck is going on here?"

Rome raised a sarcastic brow in my direction. "Yes Lexi, what is going on here."

I could kill him. I wanted to choke him with his own re-straints.

He was meant to give me time. But obviously the reminder of the danger we were facing was enough for him to throw that out the window.

I looked Colt in the eye and put on my big girl pants. "I'm pregnant."

I heard glass shatter in the kitchen.

Chapter 29

Alexis

Colt's eyes widened in astonishment as he gazed at me, his mouth agape. He seemed surprised, and asked, almost bewildered, "What?"

Hunt and Gabe suddenly appeared from the kitchen, looking shocked and surprised.

"Did I hear that correctly?" Gabe inquired, appearing stunned.

Rome, on the other hand, stood silently and watched me intently, but I couldn't read his thoughts.

"I found out earlier today," I said, my voice barely above a whisper.

Colt frowned. "You knew and you still went on the mission?"

"Yes, and if you think for a moment that I'm going to be sitting at home knitting while the big strong men do jobs you're out of your fucking mind. All that shows is that you don't know me at all. No matter how much I'm in love with you, I will take this baby and raise it my goddamn self."

A look of wonder crossed Colt's face. "You love me?" he asked, his voice filled with disbelief.

"Seriously? That's all you took from that?" I screamed in frustration and turned to walk away. He grabbed me before I even made it a step. He clasped the sides of my face, his eyes searching mine.

"We're having a baby?" he breathed, his voice barely above a whisper.

I huffed, feeling exasperated. "Well, technically, it could be one of the others'."

He shook his head firmly. "We are a family, and that's all that matters. It doesn't matter whose child it is. We're having a baby," he stated, resting his forehead against mine.

I sighed, feeling my heart begin to settle down as I smiled at him. "We're having a baby."

He leaned in to give me a gentle kiss, but then I paused and frowned at him again. "You can't stop me from going on missions with you."

He chuckled in response. "How do you feel about wearing ten layers of Kevlar around your waist?"

I smiled at him. "As long as I can still move, I'm game."

Colt threw his head back and laughed, the tension in the room dissipating. "We'll make sure to get you something that fits just right," he said, his tone playful.

I couldn't help but laugh at Colt's comment, feeling the weight of the situation lift off my shoulders. It was as if a new energy had been injected into the room and the tension had dissipated. I looked around at my men, feeling grateful for their support and love.

Rome stepped forward, a small smile playing on his lips as he curved a hand around my neck to rest his own forehead against mine where I stood in Colt's arms. "We'll make sure you're safe, Lexi. We won't let anything happen to you or the baby."

I felt a wave of emotion wash over me at his words, realizing just how much he cared for me and our child. I leaned towards him and Colt released me into his embrace, and I felt his arms wrap around me protectively.

He rubbed his cheek against my head before kissing it softly. "I love you, baby girl. I'm sorry I pushed the issue, but I don't regret it. You are so important to us and so is our baby, never doubt that."

Hunt stepped forward the moment Rome let me go and wrapped his arms around me, pulling me into a tight hug.

"You know I love you, right?" he asked, his voice low.

I smiled at him, feeling my heart swell with affection. "I know," I said. "I love you too."

"I just want you to know that I'm going to be there for you every step of the way," he said, his voice thick with emotion. "I know we're going to face some challenges, but I'm not going to let anything happen to you or our baby."

I felt tears prickle at the corners of my eyes. "Thank you," I said, my voice barely above a whisper.

Gabe wrapped his arms around me as well from behind, squeezing me between him and his brother. "I love you so much," he murmured against my hair.

"I love you too," I said, closing my eyes and breathing in their scents.

As we stood there in each other's arms, I felt a sense of peace settle over me. I knew that no matter what challenges lay ahead, we would face them together. And with these men by my side, I knew we could handle anything that came our way.

Colt pulled me from between the twins and back into a tight embrace, my back against his front, his hand resting protectively over my stomach. "I love you, princess. I can't believe we're going to be parents," he murmured against my hair.

I smiled up at him, feeling overwhelmed with love for these men who had become my world in every sense of the word. "Me neither," I replied softly. "But we're going to be amazing parents."

Colt nodded, his eyes sparkling with emotion. "We are. And we're going to make sure our baby has the best life possible."

I couldn't help but feel relieved they seemed to be taking the news of the baby in stride. I had been worried that they would be angry or resentful, but instead they seemed excited about the prospect of becoming fathers. But there was still a big issue.

My smile slipped away. "How can we while Dominick is still chasing me?"

"We won't let him get to you, princess."

"He thinks I belong to him, that I'm his. His to abuse and his to kill when he wants."

"No!" he shouted before he turned me around and pulled me into him tighter, breathing in the scent of my hair as he calmed his temper. "Make no mistake, you are ours. We are in this. All of us. There is no going back for us, no saying goodbye once this asshole is dead. Our hearts, they beat for you. We would love and die for you. You are our Queen."

He gripped the hair at the back of my head as he raised his face to look at me intensely. "From the moment I saw you I knew you would be our Queen. You were made for us. But I knew none of us were there yet. So you became my Princess instead, waiting for the day you took your rightful place beside us."

Tears came to my eyes as his words registered and I leaned up to kiss Colt again, feeling the weight of the world lift off my shoulders for the first time in what felt like forever. Whatever Dominick planned for us, we would face it together, as a family.

And as I stood there in Colt's arms, surrounded by the people I loved most in the world, I knew that nothing could ever tear us apart.

Chapter 30

Colt

I was going to be a father.

My mind was completely blown at the revelation.

I managed to steal Lexi away into my room where I was wrapped around her beautiful body in bed with my face nestled in her neck and our legs tangled together.

I knew I needed to tell her my story, but it was just so hard to talk about. The past wasn't something I liked to look at.

She must have felt the tension in me because she moved away to look at my face, her soft fingers brushing over my forehead where I had been frowning without realizing it.

"What's wrong?" She asked me softly and I closed my eyes for a moment, just to appreciate her touch.

"Did Ash ever tell you about her family?" I asked, looking back into her gorgeous hazel eyes.

She shook her head slightly in response. "No, we kind of kept most things pretty surface level because of how we met. I didn't even know she had any brothers."

I sighed, reaching up to brush a strand of hair from her face as I gathered myself to tell her. "Our dad died when we were young, Ash was only a few years old, I was only five. He had a heart attack while he slept, and simply didn't wake up in the morning."

She looked at me sadly but didn't interrupt.

"My mom tried to cope as best she could. She started working two jobs just to provide for us. She managed to keep us in a mostly decent house in a semi-decent neighborhood. But she worked her ass off to do it. When I was older, I tried my best to help, taking little odd jobs with the neighbors, and looking back at it, it was almost laughable that I thought the occasional ten to twenty dollars would make a difference." I smiled softly at the memory.

"Ten years after my dad died my mom started seeing this guy. He seemed nice enough, he had money, showered all of us with gifts and paid our rent so mom didn't have to work so much. But there was just something about him that didn't feel right." I frowned thinking back on that time and Lexi smoothed a finger down my forehead again before cradling a hand against my face, silently offering me her support.

"I was about fifteen at the time, and no matter what I said to mom about how I felt she wouldn't listen to me. Even Ash was scared of him, but since I had been the one who mostly raised her, she wouldn't say anything to mom about how she felt. And then completely out of the blue mom tells us she's pregnant. She was already a few months along but hadn't said anything until she started to show because she knew she couldn't hide it from us anymore." I heard her breath catch at that and I nuzzled my face into her hand, smoothing one of mine down her back until I felt her settle again.

"They started fighting pretty regularly after that. Actual screaming matches that had the neighbors calling the cops. We found out very quickly at that point that the cops wouldn't do anything about him. It turned out he was part of the local mafia. And what's worse was that he already had a family.. We were just entertainment to him, a distraction from his traditional Italian wife and his traditional Italian life." She frowned as I saw a touch of rage enter her face and I knew she was thinking of Dominick.

I took a few moments to breathe through the memories of what came next. "Mom was about eight months pregnant when they got into a huge fight. Ash and I were so scared when we heard them start screaming at each other. We had found the best hiding spot one of the previous times in a little hidden panel in my closet so we both crawled in there to hide and just held each other. It wasn't long before the argument-turned into mom screaming for her life. We heard every detail as he beat her and then stabbed her to death. And as though that wasn't enough, even though she was already dead, he then shot her in her head and then her stomach."

Lexi brushed her fingers against my cheek and it's only at that moment that I noticed the tears that glistened on her fingers, matching the ones sliding down her own cheeks. "The doctors said that they might have been able to rescue the baby if they had been quick enough and if he hadn't put a bullet in her stomach. He tried to look for me and Ash too, he tore the house apart looking for us, but we managed to stay hidden until he ran away at the first sign of sirens."

I took a deep breath, feeling the weight of the memory heavy on my chest. Lexi's hand never left my face, her touch grounding me as I continued. I hugged Lexi tightly to me, her tears wetting my shirt, and I could feel the weight of the memories crashing down on me again.

"They managed to track him down pretty quickly and he died while resisting arrest. After that we were put into the foster care system. We bounced around for a little while, but thankfully stayed together until we were put into a good foster home. That's where we met Nix and the guys."

Lexi's face was full of empathy and understanding as she listened to my story. I could feel her love and support radiating off of her as she held me close. "I'm so sorry," she whispered softly. "I can't even imagine what that must have been like for you and Ash."

I smiled sadly at her. "It was rough, but we had each other. And we got through it together."

"Is that why you do what you do? To help others like your mom?" Lexi asked, her eyes searching mine.

I nodded. "Yeah, I wanted to be able to protect people who couldn't protect themselves. And I wanted to make sure no one had to go through what we did."

Lexi leaned in and pressed her lips to mine in a soft kiss, her hands running through my hair. "I'm so proud of you," she whispered against my lips. "You're such an amazing person."

I felt my heart swell with love for her as I wrapped my arms tighter around her. "I'm just me, but I'm glad I have you in my life."

We stayed wrapped up in each other's arms for a while longer, just holding each other and processing everything that had happened.

"I don't know how to be a dad," I admitted softly to Lexi. "I barely know how to be an adult some days."

She smiled softly at me. "We'll figure it out together. It's not just us, we're a team, remember that. We will all work together to make sure this baby is completely loved and protected from the horrors of the world."

I nodded, feeling a little more hopeful. "Yeah, you're right. We'll do it together."

As we lay there in each other's arms drifting off to sleep, I felt a sense of peace wash over me. I knew it wouldn't be easy, but with Lexi by my side, I knew we could handle anything that came our way.

Chapter 31

Alexis

O nce again the following morning the twins stole me to go shopping. This time for a charity masquerade gala they were planning to attend in honor of Colt's mom.

I was thankful he told me his story. If I hadn't already been in love with him, that would have definitely tipped me over the edge.

We were approaching a high end dress store when a thought occurred to me. "This isn't just another excuse to have sex with me in public is it?" I asked, looking at Gabe suspiciously.

He looked at me with exaggerated wide eyes. "Would we do that?"

I chuckled as I shook my head. "Well it seems almost like a trend or competition at this point."

They both stopped suddenly and turned towards me with their mouths dropped open. "Umm, please explain that," Hunt said in a disbelieving tone as I paused and looked at them.

I felt the heat flame across my face and my own eyes widened as I realized they didn't know about my trip to the library.

I cleared my throat and started towards the store again. "So tell me more about this gala."

I heard them laugh as they rushed to catch up to me, each taking one of my arms to pull me to a stop. "Ahh, no, you aren't getting away with that." Gabe said, grinning at me.

I rolled my eyes and ducked my head down as the memory came back. "Well, Colt and Rome showed me around town the other day. Including the library. And the stacks at the back of the library." I let the last part hang in the air.

They bursted out laughing. I couldn't stop the grin that pulled at my lips at the sound, even with my cheeks flaming.

Hunt shook his head. "Okay, you are absolutely going to give us more details than that, but that can wait till later," he said before stepping into me and lowering his voice. "Maybe while you're slowly riding my cock."

Fuck, there they go again being all hot. No wonder I was pregnant.

They were still chuckling softly as they both hooked their arms in mine and escorted me into the store.

As we walked through the store, I couldn't help but feel overwhelmed by the beautiful dresses and the prices that came along with them. Gabe and Hunt lead me towards a section filled with elegant and colorful gowns.

I spent the next hour trying on various dresses, each one more beautiful than the last. I started to feel like a princess as the twins fussed over me, adjusting the hemlines and smoothing out any wrinkles.

"This one," Gabe declared as he stepped back to admire his handiwork. "This is the one."

I looked at myself in the mirror and gasped. The dress was a stunning emerald green color, hugging my curves in all the right places. It had a deep V-neckline and a flowing skirt that trailed behind me as I twirled.

"It's perfect," I said, feeling a little emotional.

Hunt came up behind me and wrapped his arms around my waist, resting his chin on my shoulder. "You look absolutely breathtaking," he whispered in my ear.

I turned my head to kiss him softly on the lips, feeling grateful and overwhelmed by their love and attention.

Looking back towards the mirror I watched as his hands slid down to rest against my stomach gently. "I still can't believe we made this," he said, his voice filled with wonder and amazement.

I smiled at him, feeling tears prickle at the corners of my eyes. "I know. It's still hard for me to believe too."

Gabe stepped up beside us and wrapped his arms around both of us. "Well, we're going to make sure this little one has the best life possible," he said, pressing a kiss to the top of my head.

I leaned into them both, feeling the overwhelming love and happiness radiating from them. It's a feeling I never wanted to let go of.

After we purchased the dress and a few accessories to go with it, we headed back to the house. The Gala wasn't for another few days so we had the rest of the day to just relax.

As we settled on the couch together to watch a movie, I felt their eyes on me as I snuggled between them. "So, about those details..." Gabe started, a mischievous glint in his eye.

I rolled my eyes playfully. "You really want to hear about that?"

Hunt leaned in and kissed me softly. "Of course we do. We want to know everything."

I felt my cheeks as they warmed up again and took a deep breath. "Well, according to Colt, you both need to up your game," I said with a chuckle.

Their incredulous protests were so loud they echoed around the room and had me throwing my head back in laughter.

Suddenly Gabe grabbed the back of my neck, pulling me until my face was inches from his. The look in his eyes was an intense smoldering fire. "Up our game huh?"

I choked on the laughter, my breath caught at the intensity with which he spoke.

He stood up, dragging me from the couch as he did. "Turn that fucking tv off, seems we have a challenge to answer," he snarled at Hunt before we were suddenly moving. He pulled me by the hand behind him up the stairs. I stumbled slightly in his haste and Hunt's hands grabbed my hips to steady me as he growled at his brother to be careful.

Gabe led us into his own room this time. "Leave the door open, let those assholes hear," he said over his shoulder to Hunt.

When he reached the foot of his bed he spun around, grabbed the sides of my neck and crashed his lips onto mine. I clutched at his shirt as he flicked his tongue against my lips, my own mouth opening automatically for him so he could plunge his tongue into my mouth. I loved the feeling of his piercing against my tongue, the hard coldness adding that extra thrill and making me moan into his mouth. He moved a hand down to wrap around my throat, not squeezing but still enough to have me heating up.

He drew back from me and his eyes were intense. "Do you remember my promise to you the day before you were taken from us?"

I flinched as my mind took me straight to the awful memories of being taken to Nick and what came after. Gabe's hand tightened around my neck as he brought my forehead against his.

"No, you're not to think about the time in between ever again. Do you remember the promise I made to you while I was fucking you on Hunt's bed?"

Heat instantly flared across my cheeks at the memory and I nodded my head slightly against his.

He brushed his lips against mine again and pulled his face further away. "What did I promise, beautiful?"

I was panting at the mere thought. "That you would fuck my ass while I rode Hunt, and then you would cum on me to mark me as yours." My voice was a husky rasp, I was so turned on. The hot and possessive look in his eyes burned into my very soul.

He slid his tongue against his bottom lip, the piercing glinting in the light. "Let's get you warmed up, beautiful."

He stripped me of my clothes and turned me around. Hunt stood behind me gloriously naked, his hand is fisted around his cock, turning and sliding along its length until he squeezed the tip before sliding back down to the base.

My mouth watered at the sight.

"Kneel. I want to see you choke on his cock." Gabe growled into my ear, his hands pressed down on my shoulders and I eagerly dropped to my knees to obey his orders.

Hunt stepped forward as I looked up the long line of his body and into his eyes from where I was kneeling before him. The look he gave me was pure hunger. Like a wolf looking at its prey.

Hunt's cock was hard and pulsing in front of me, and I couldn't wait to taste him. I slowly leaned forward and watched him as I ran my tongue slowly up the underside of his cock from where he had a tight grip on it to swirl around the head teasingly. I watched as he bit onto his lip as he groaned.

Even on my knees for him I felt like the most powerful woman in the world.

Gabe threaded his hand into my hair and gripped a handful as he crouched down behind me, I could feel his naked skin against mine and knew he had shed his clothes while I was distracted with Hunt. "Open," he growled sharply in my ear and the moment my mouth dropped open he pushed me forward until Hunt's cock was buried in my throat.

Gabe's hand tightened in my hair, keeping my head where it was and I moaned loudly in response. Hunt cursed from above me, his hips drawing back slightly to allow me to breathe.

I moved to bring my hands up to wrap around the base of Hunt's cock, but Gabe quickly released my hair to capture my hands and drag them behind my back. I felt something slip around my wrists and tighten before Gabe leaned into me. "Is that ok, beautiful?" he asked and my heart gave a squeeze at the thoughtful question.

I nodded as best I could with Hunt's cock still in my mouth.

He rubbed his face against mine briefly before licking the shell of my ear. "Good, because Hunt is going to fuck that pretty mouth while I warm you up."

Fuck.

Chapter 32

Alexis

Hunt's hand replaced his brother's gripping my hair as Gabe disappeared from behind me. "Open that pretty throat again for me sweetheart."

I complied eagerly, feeling Hunt's cock slide further into my mouth again as I relaxed my throat muscles, allowing him to push in deeper. I felt his fingers tighten in my hair as he started to thrust, his cock moving in and out of my mouth, each stroke hitting the back of my throat. I moaned around him, the vibration making him groan again above me.

I felt when Gabe returned and knelt behind me. His hands started to roam over my back, caressing my skin and pushing me forward and further onto Hunt's cock. The added pressure on my back made me choke slightly when Hunt's cock pushed further down my throat at this new angle. His nails scraped down my spine and made my whole body shiver as I gasped around Hunt's cock.

"Fuck her throat, Hunt," Gabe commanded. "Make her gag on that cock."

He stopped touching me for a moment as he did something behind me. Hunt's hands tightened in my hair and his thrusts became harsher, pushing even further down my throat, my nose brushing his pelvis with each thrust.

When Gabe's hands returned he reached around to grip my throat again with one hand while his other went in the opposite direction. He squeezed my throat, bending me into a harsh arch. I felt his wet finger circling my rear entrance slowly and I realized he went and got lube.

My body tensed at the touch, but Gabe's hand on my throat kept me grounded. I moaned loudly around Hunt's cock as Gabe's finger pushed slowly inside me, the lube making it slick and easy to slide in. He slowly pulled it back out before thrusting it into my ass again. He added a second finger, scissoring them inside me, stretching me, and preparing me for what was to come.

"Such a good fucking girl for us," Gabe murmured into my ear, his hand still on my throat.

I could feel Hunt's cock twitching as he thrust into my throat, his breathing becoming more ragged as he got closer to the edge. Gabe's fingers moved faster, hitting that spot inside me that made my whole body tremble.

"You want more, don't you?" Gabe's voice was a whisper in my ear, his breath hot against my skin. "You want my cock in your ass, filling you up while Hunt fucks that pretty wet pussy of yours."

I moaned around Hunt's cock, my pussy throbbing at his words as I nodded eagerly.

Suddenly, Gabe withdrew his fingers, leaving me feeling empty and wanting more. I whimpered, but the sound was muffled by Hunt's cock still filling my throat. Gabe chuckled behind me, the sound low and dark.

Gabe's hand left my throat and I gasped for air, feeling Hunt's cock slide out of my mouth. Gabe stood and pulled me up by my hair, turning me to face him. I could see the lust in his eyes as he looked at me.

"You're so fucking beautiful," Gabe growled, his hands running down my body, cupping my breasts and pinching my nipples hard. My arms were still bound behind me, not allowing me to offer any resistance to his attention. "We're gonna fuck you so hard, you won't be able to walk straight for a week."

My pussy clenched at his words, and I moaned in anticipation. I could feel Hunt's eyes on me as well, watching us with hunger.

Gabe moved around behind me and then used my bound arms to move me over to where Hunt was sitting on the edge of the bed stroking his hard cock. They worked together to help me straddle Hunt's lap, positioning me so that his cock was pressing against my wet and eager pussy. I let out a whimper as I felt him push inside me, filling me up completely as they pushed me down.

Hunt's hands were on my hips, guiding me as I started to ride him, my body moving up and down on his cock.

"Ride him, beautiful. Show him who you belong to," Gabe growled into my ear.

I moaned in response, my body already on fire. I began to move faster, riding Hunt's cock harder, my pussy clenching around him. I could feel Hunt's hands gripping my hips tightly, pulling me down harder onto his cock as he matched my rhythm.

I heard the sound of Gabe opening the lube again and then felt his fingers spreading it over my ass.

He slowly circled his fingers around my entrance, teasing me before pushing one finger inside me again. I moaned loudly as I felt the stretch, my body adjusting quicker this time to the intrusion. Gabe added a second finger, scissoring them inside me just like before, preparing me.

I whimpered when he added a third, my rhythm on Hunt's cock faltering to a stop as he thrust his fingers into my ass.

My body was aching for more, and I pushed back against his fingers, silently begging for him to take me. Gabe's hand left my ass, and I could hear him moving around behind me. He pushed me forward onto Hunt's chest as he laid down and Hunt took advantage by gripping my hair. He pulled me into a deep and dirty kiss, his tongue mimicking what his cock had just been doing to my pussy.

More lube dripped onto my ass, sliding down to where Hunt was buried in me. I shivered at the coolness of the lube.

"I need to feel that tight little ass wrapped around my cock." Gabe rasped into my ear and suddenly, I felt the head of his cock pressing against my entrance. I gasped as he slowly pushed inside me and I cried out into Hunt's mouth, feeling the stretch and burn as he filled me up completely. His piercing added to the sensation.

I could feel every inch of Gabe's hard cock as he slowly began to move inside me, stretching me wider than I had ever been before, his piercing hitting all the right spots. Hunt's hands were gripping my hair tightly, holding me still as Gabe began to pick up the pace, thrusting deeper and harder into my ass. I moaned, the sensation of being completely filled by both of them overwhelming me. The pleasure and pain were intermingling, making me feel like I was losing control of my body.

Gabe wrapped a hand around my throat from behind, pulling me up and away from Hunt, making my back arch and pressing my bound arms between our bodies.

My mind was a blur of sensations, and I could barely keep up with everything that was happening to me. Hunt's hands moved from my hair to my breasts, pinching and pulling on my nipples as Gabe's cock continued to stretch me wide open.

I could feel myself getting closer and closer to the edge, my body trembling with need. Gabe's hand tightened around my throat, cutting off my air even more as both of them thrust into me harder and faster.

"That's it, beautiful. Take it all. Take both of our cocks like the good fucking girl you are," Gabe growled, his breath hot against my ear.

I moaned, feeling the pleasure and desire take over my body. "Yes, please, I want both of your cocks," I rasped back, my voice filled with need. "I want to be your good girl."

Hunt pushed himself back up so he was pressed against the front of my body again. His hands returned to my hips to lift me up so that he could start thrusting his cock deep into my pussy. They found a rhythm between themselves, one of them thrusting hard inside me as the other retreated.

My body was an inferno, the pleasure building out of control with every thrust. The sound of skin slapping against skin echoed through the room as they both fucked me hard. I could feel the pressure building inside me low in my belly.

As Hunt pounded into me, his cock hitting my g-spot with every thrust, Gabe's hand left my throat and moved to grip my hair tightly. He pulled me back, forcing me to arch my back even more, and I cried out at the sensation.

"You love this, don't you? You love being our little fuck toy," Gabe growled, his other hand reaching around to pinch and twist my nipples. "You're such a dirty girl for taking both of our cocks like this."

"Yes, I love it. I want both of your cocks. I want to be your dirty little toy, filled and fucked by you both," I moaned in response, my body craving more of their touch.

Hunt's hands were now gripping my ass, pulling me down onto his cock harder as Gabe continued to stretch me open with his own.

"That's it, take it all," Hunt grunted, his thrusts becoming more urgent. "Take our cocks like the good fucking girl you are."

"Please, I'm so close," I begged, my voice hoarse with need. "I need to cum, please let me cum for you."

As I felt the heat building up inside me and the familiar pressure low in my belly, my body trembled on the brink of orgasm. Gabe must have sensed it too because he leaned in close to my ear and whispered, "Let go for us, beautiful. Drench this fucking bed."

Hunt grunted and thrust harder, his movements becoming more erratic as he chased his own release. "Squeeze my cock with that tight little pussy. Cum for us."

With those words, my body convulsed, and I screamed as my orgasm ripped through me. My pussy clenched hard, forcing out Hunt's cock, and I felt a gush of cum drenching Hunt and the bed as Gabe pulled out of my ass and lifted me off Hunt.

Gabe dropped me onto my knees beside the bed as they both moved to stand in front of me stroking their hard and throbbing cocks.

I panted heavily, still lost in the aftermath of my orgasm, as I looked up at them.

Gabe and Hunt were both towering over me, their muscular bodies glistening with sweat. Their eyes were dark with lust as they watched me with hungry gazes. I couldn't help but feel powerful for being able to turn these two men into feral animals, it turned me on beyond belief.

Gabe reached down and grabbed a fistful of my hair, pulling my head back to expose my neck. "Open your mouth," he commanded, his voice low and demanding.

Without hesitation, I parted my lips. He squeezed and stroked his cock, strangling it with his own hand. "You want my cum, dirty girl? You want me to paint your face with my cum and mark you as ours?"

"Please," I begged, my eyes locked onto his as he continued to stroke himself.

Gabe's strokes became faster and more erratic as he approached his own release. "Open wide, no swallowing until we say you can," he ordered, and I did as I was told, sticking my tongue out to catch the first hot splash of his cum on my tongue and face as he moaned low, continuing to stroke his cock until he was finished.

Hunt stepped forward, his throbbing cock in his hand, and I turned my mouth towards him, craving his release. "You want my cum too, sweetheart?" he taunted, his voice low and rough. "You want me to shoot my hot load all over your eager tongue and pretty face?" I whimpered, nodding eagerly as he aimed his cock at my open mouth and he let out a low growl as he exploded all over my tongue and face. I moaned as his hot cum filled my mouth, and I kept it there, savoring the taste and waiting for their permission to swallow. There was so much that it started to drip down onto my chest.

Gabe and Hunt exchanged a look, then nodded to each other. "Swallow," they said in unison, and I eagerly obeyed, feeling their satisfaction as I swallowed it down.

Their eyes burned into me as I stuck my tongue out to show them I was done. Gabe tutted at me as he crouched down, his fingers scooping up the cum that had dripped onto my chest, gathering it up and then thrusting his fingers into my mouth.

"Clean yourself up, dirty girl," he growled, his voice rough with desire as I obediently sucked his fingers clean. Hunt stepped behind me, his hands threading through my hair as he leaned down to whisper in my ear. "You did such a good job, sweetheart," he praised, his breath hot against my skin.

Gabe helped me stand back up and Hunt released my hands, both of them taking one of my wrists in their hands to rub at my skin. I shivered at the touch of their hands on me while my body still hummed with pleasure. They seemed to know exactly what I needed, and I felt so completely taken care of and satisfied.

Gabe leaned down to kiss me, his lips soft and gentle against mine, a stark contrast to the roughness of our earlier actions.

Hunt brushed his lips against my neck as he gently wrapped an arm around my waist, his hand going to my stomach automatically. "Let's go have a shower and get cleaned up. Promise we won't ravage you in the shower this time," he said, laughing softly.

Chapter 33

Hunt

After Gabe and I took our time cleaning Lexi in the shower and making sure she was okay we moved to my room to cuddle her between us in my bed.

I lazily stroked a hand down her side, savoring the softness of her skin as she molded her body against me. Gabe was on her other side playing gently with her hair, running it through his fingers and wrapping it around his hand before releasing it over and over again.

The room was quiet except for the sound of our breathing, and I felt a sense of peace settle over us. It was as if we were in our own little bubble, isolated from the rest of the world.

I shifted my gaze to Gabe, who was watching Lexi with an expression of adoration. I knew his thoughts were still half on the encounter that we just had with her, and honestly, who could blame him? My thoughts however moved in a different direction.

As I continued to lazily stroke a hand down Lexi's side, my thoughts drifted to the past. It was hard to believe that just a few years ago, Gabe and I were serving in the military.

First our parents died in a car accident right after we were deployed and then we were being taken advantage of and used by the wrong people. It was a dark time in our lives, one that we rarely talked about.

I remembered the constant sense of danger and fear that hung over us every day, the sleepless nights filled with nightmares, and the endless parade of death and destruction that we witnessed. It was a bleak existence, one that left us feeling hollow and disconnected from the rest of the world.

When Colt rescued us from that bad situation, we thought that we could just go back to our normal lives, but we quickly realized that it was impossible. We were different people, scarred and broken by our experiences. We struggled to adjust at first, and we felt like we didn't fit in anywhere.

Even after spending so much time with Colt and Rome, we weren't completely back to the place we had been before the military. To the happy and fun boys that we were prior to enlisting. Despite our efforts to move on, our past still haunted us. It manifested in different ways, in the nightmares that still plagued us, in the anxiety attacks that would hit us unexpectedly, and in the pervasive feeling of sadness that we couldn't seem to shake off.

Then, Lexi came into our lives.

I felt a sense of contentment knowing that we had found something special in each other. She was a ray of sunshine, a burst of energy that brought light into our darkness. Our dynamic was unique and not for everyone, but it worked for us. We were a team, a family, and I couldn't imagine my life without them.

As I gazed down at Lexi's peaceful face, I couldn't help but feel a sense of protectiveness wash over me. We had been through so much together already, and I was determined to make sure that nothing ever harmed her again.

She must have noticed a shift in my mood because she looked over at me with concern in her eyes. "You okay?" she asked softly.

I nodded, not trusting myself to speak. Instead, I pressed a gentle kiss to her forehead and whispered, "I love you."

She smiled softly. "I love you too."

As I held Lexi in my arms, I couldn't help but feel grateful for everything she had brought into our lives. "Lexi," I began, "I want to tell you something."

She looked up at me, her beautiful hazel eyes shining with curiosity. "What is it?" she asked.

"You have no idea how much you've changed our lives," I said, my voice filled with emotion. "Before you came into our world, things were... different. Gabe and I were living our lives, but we weren't really living. We were just going through the motions."

Lexi's brow furrowed, and I could tell she didn't understand what I meant. I took a deep breath and continued, "But now that you're with us, everything is different. We laugh more, we tease more, we smile easier, and we sleep better. You have brought so much light and joy into our lives, and we love you for it."

Gabe nodded in agreement, his expression softening as he looked at Lexi. "We are so lucky to have you," he said, his voice barely above a whisper. "You make everything better."

Lexi's eyes filled with tears, and she looked at us with so much love that it felt like my heart was going to burst. "I love you both so much," she said, her voice choked with emotion. "You've changed my life too."

As we held each other in a tight embrace, I knew that we were all thinking the same thing: that we were lucky to have found each other, and that nothing would ever tear us apart.

Moving out of the embrace I slide down the bed to gently kiss her stomach. Even though she was only three weeks along, our baby was already starting to grow inside her.

It was only the size of a tiny seed but that didn't matter to me.

She threaded a hand through my hair softly as I rubbed my face against her skin.

"This baby is going to be so loved. They will never once know the darkness that we have experienced in our lives." I said softly.

She hums contentedly. "I know they will."

As I snuggled against Lexi's stomach, I felt her fingers play with my hair, and I couldn't help but smile. "So, what do you think we should name the little one?" I asked, glancing up at her.

She raised an eyebrow. "Oh, you're asking me now?" she said with a playful smirk. "I thought you guys probably had it all figured out already."

Gabe chuckled. "We have a few ideas," he admitted, running a hand up and down her arm. "But we thought we'd give you a chance to weigh in."

Lexi pretended to consider it for a moment. "Hmm, let's see," she said, tapping her chin thoughtfully. "How about... Spaghetti?"

I snorted. "Spaghetti? You want to name our child after a pasta dish?"

She shrugged. "Hey, I'm just brainstorming here. You never know, it could catch on. And if I recall correctly, you do have a thing for food."

My laughter echoed around the room and it took us a moment before we settled back down again.

Gabe was still chuckling as he said, "Yeah, I'm not so sure about that one. What about something a little more traditional? Like... Michael or Elizabeth?"

Lexi wrinkled her nose. "Boring," she teased. "We need something more unique. How about... River? We can't have Phoenix since we already have one of those in the family... Ooh, what about Luna?"

I smiled. "Luna's not bad. I kind of like that one."

Gabe nodded in agreement. "Luna's a pretty name. I could see us calling her Luna."

Lexi grinned triumphantly. "See? I knew I could come up with something good. Or ooh what about Raven, that's a strong girl's name. Our kid is going to be a badass, just like us."

I rolled my eyes. "Well, we'll see. We've still got a few months to decide."

"Months?" Lexi repeated, feigning shock. "Oh no, I thought we were going to decide right now. What are we going to do for the next few months?"

Gabe chuckled. "I'm sure we'll find plenty of other things to occupy our time."

I smirked. "Yeah, like preparing for the arrival of our little Spaghetti."

Lexi groaned. "Don't even joke about that," she said, swatting playfully at my arm. "I refuse to have a child named after food."

I chuckled. "Alright, alright, we'll keep looking. I'm sure we will come up with something pretty. If it's a girl."

Gabe nodded again. "And if we can't make up our minds, we can always go with Spaghetti."

Lexi rolled her eyes. "I'm never going to hear the end of that, am I?" she said, shaking her head with a smile. "You two are impossible."

We all laughed, and for a moment, everything felt perfect. As we laid there, snuggled up together, I knew that no matter what the future held, we would face it together.

Gradually Lexi drifted off to sleep, her breathing slow and even.

Gabe and I laid there for a while longer, lost in our own thoughts, until Gabe spoke up again. "Do you ever worry about the future?" he asked quietly.

I turned to look at him, surprised by the question. "What do you mean?"

"I mean, with everything that's happened in our lives, do you ever worry that we won't be able to give our child the life they deserve? That we're too damaged and won't be good parents?"

I took a deep breath, considering his words. "Sometimes," I admitted. "But then I remember how far we've come. We've been through so much, and we've come out the other side. We're strong, and we have the love of a beautiful woman to guide us. We aren't alone in this, we have Colt and Rome also. We'll make sure our baby always feels love and has everything they need."

Gabe nodded slowly, his eyes locked onto mine. "You're right," he said, his voice filled with determination. "We will. We'll give them the best life possible, and we'll do it together."

I smiled, "Together," I repeated. "That's all that matters."

As the night wore on and we eventually drifted off to sleep, I couldn't help but feel a sense of excitement for the future. Our lives had been transformed in ways we never could have imagined, and it was all thanks to the woman in our arms. And as we continued to grow and change and face whatever came our way, I knew that we would always have each other, and that was all that mattered.

Chapter 34

Alexis

The next afternoon Colt decided we were going to go out to dinner as a family.

Excited about the prospect of having dinner all together, we all went our separate ways to get ready. I chose a nice pair of black pants and a loose brown blouse to hide the gun I had holstered underneath.

Standing in front of the mirror I smoothed the blouse down and made sure you couldn't tell what I was hiding. My hand brushed over my lower stomach and my breath caught for a moment thinking about the life growing in there.

I took a deep breath and shook off the momentary feeling of anxiety. This was supposed to be a special evening with my family, and I didn't want my nerves to ruin it.

As we got into Colt's car and started driving, I felt a sense of excitement building up inside me. I couldn't wait to try the food at the restaurant Colt had chosen and spend quality time with my loved ones.

When we arrived, Colt held the door open for me and I stepped inside, the cool air of the air-conditioning washing over me. I was relieved to see that the lighting was dim and the music was soft.

As we settled into our cozy booth toward the back, Colt started pouring us some table water and he glanced over at me with a playful grin. "So, are you excited to try the food here? It's supposed to be amazing."

I grinned back at him, feeling a sense of anticipation. "Definitely. I've been craving some good Italian food lately."

Hunt chuckled. "I hope this isn't you starting to blame the baby for bad eating habits."

I laughed at Hunt's playful comment. "No way, I take full responsibility for my cravings. But hey, at least I have a good excuse now."

Colt grinned. "And we're more than happy to indulge your cravings, no matter how weird they may be."

Gabe nodded in agreement. "Yeah, just let us know what you're in the mood for and we'll make it happen."

I felt a surge of gratitude towards my men. "Thanks, guys. I really appreciate it. And speaking of cravings, can we order some garlic knots to start?"

Rome grinned. "Garlic knots it is. And maybe we should also get some calamari and bruschetta to share?"

Hunt raised his glass. "I'll drink to that."

As we perused the menu and placed our orders, I felt a sense of contentment wash over me. Being surrounded by my loved ones, sharing a meal and enjoying each other's company, was all I could ask for.

When the food arrived, we dug in eagerly, savoring every bite. The garlic knots were warm and doughy, the calamari was crispy and perfectly seasoned, and the bruschetta was bursting with fresh tomato flavor.

As we chatted and laughed and enjoyed our meal, I felt a sense of happiness and belonging. These men were my family, my support system, and I knew that no matter what challenges lay ahead, we would face them together.

As we made our way towards the car after dinner, I paused for a moment. Something felt off. When something felt off I always trusted my gut in these situations. It was usually right.

I stood still in the middle of the sidewalk and the guys stopped a step in front of me to look towards me curiously. Hunt picked up on it first, quickly narrowing his eyes to look around the narrow street. Colt and Gabe also started looking around while Rome edged closer to me.

"What's wrong?" Colt asked.

"I don't know," I said, scanning the area around us. "I just have a feeling something's not right."

Hunt put his hand on my shoulder, his grip firm and reassuring. "Trust your instincts, sweetheart. If something feels off, it probably is."

As if on cue, a group of men appeared from around a van that was parked close to our car, weapons aimed at us. There were three of them. We weren't outnumbered, but while our weapons were all holstered we were unfortunately outgunned.

"We were having such a good day! Why did you have to go and ruin it?" Hunt snarked at them.

The leader of the group stepped forward, a smug grin on his face as he addressed us.

"Give us the girl and nobody has to get hurt," he said, his voice laced with a thick accent.

I reached for my weapon, but one of the men shouted at us to keep our hands where they could see them. Colt, Gabe, and Hunt had their hands up, but they all had a look of steely determination in their eyes. Rome stepped in front of me, shielding me with his body.

The men approached us, and I could see the cold, calculating look in their eyes. They were professionals. They knew what they were doing. I felt a sense of dread wash over me, but I tried to remain calm.

Suddenly, I heard footsteps behind us. I turned my head and saw another group of men had silently approached us from the other direction. They were also armed, and they looked just as dangerous as the first group. The leader of the new group reached out to grab my arm.

Suddenly, Rome sprang into action, moving with lightning-fast speed as he appeared beside the man reaching for me and took him out with a swift, brutal snap of his neck. "Don't touch her," he snarled.

The other men hesitated for a moment, stunned by the sudden violence, and that was all the time we needed.

In a flash, the guys drew their weapons and opened fire, taking down the remaining attackers in a hail of bullets. The sound of gunfire echoed through the narrow street, and I felt a sense of relief wash over me as the last attacker fell to the ground mere seconds later.

Wow, what a dinner outing. Nothing said family bonding like a group of armed men trying to kidnap you in the middle of the street and the men you loved killing said group. I bet that's a memory we will all cherish forever.

"Well, that was unexpected," I said, my heart racing as I tried to catch my breath.

Hunt wrapped his arm around my shoulders, his grip tight and reassuring. "Are you okay?" he asked, concern etched into his features.

I nodded, still in shock at what had just happened. "Yeah, I'm okay. Thanks to you guys."

Colt stepped forward, his weapon still drawn as he scanned the area around us for any more threats. "Let's get out of here," he said, his voice steady and calm.

We quickly made our way back to the car, all of us on high alert. As we drove away from the scene, I couldn't help but think about how lucky we had been. If it hadn't been for Rome's quick moves and the guys' expertise with weapons, things could have gone very differently.

I leaned my head back against the seat, my mind racing as I tried to process what just happened. Despite the danger we just faced, I couldn't help but feel a sense of pride and admiration for the men in my life. They were strong, skilled, and fiercely protective of our family.

It was clear that they would do anything to keep us safe, even putting their own lives on the line. I knew that I was lucky to have them by my side, and that thought brought a sense of comfort amidst the chaos of the situation.

As we arrived back home, we all gathered in the living room, still feeling the effects from the events of the night.

Adrenaline was still coursing through me making me edgy, I paced the floor feeling twitchy. I brushed my hands against my abdomen, thankful we were all safe.

It wasn't long before someone pulled me to a stop and stepped up behind me, arms sliding around my waist to rest over mine as his body molded to my back. "So, have you forgiven me?" Rome asked quietly, brushing his cheek against my hair before placing a gentle kiss on my temple.

I looked at him with wide eyes. "There's nothing to forgive." I insisted.

He raised a brow in response. "I forced you to tell everyone before you were ready."

I shook my head. "You were right, I needed to tell everyone. I was just afraid of how they would react, that the baby would be yet another obligation that was thrown at you. Like I was."

He frowned deeply and narrowed his eyes at me. "What did I tell you, baby girl? What did I say would happen next time you dismissed yourself and our feelings for you."

My stomach dropped. Fuck.

Of course I remembered the conversation he was talking about.

He tilted his head as he watched me. "I asked you a question, baby girl."

I swallowed as heat flared across my cheeks. "You would turn my ass red," I whispered.

Colt chuckled, "I didn't quite hear that, princess."

I closed my eyes. "Rome said he would turn my ass red and you all agreed to watch."

Rome hummed in satisfaction. "That's right, baby girl. And what did you just do?"

I peeked up at him through my lashes. "I dismissed myself and didn't listen to what you were telling me."

He hummed again in approval against my ear. "That's right, baby girl. So, you know what that means."

I knew exactly what that meant. I bit my lip, feeling a mixture of arousal and apprehension. I knew I shouldn't be turned on by the thought of being punished, but I couldn't help it.

And with all the adrenaline still moving through me I knew this was what I needed. And I knew they knew that too.

"Strip for us," Rome ordered, his voice low and commanding.

I nodded, knowing that I had no choice but to comply. With shaking hands, I began to undress, feeling their eyes on me the entire time. When I was naked, Rome brushed a hand down the length of my arm before he took my hand and led me to the couch.

"Kneel on the lounge, arms on the back," he commanded.

I did as he ordered, my heart pounding in my chest as I knelt on the couch facing the back with my forearms resting on the backrest. Colt came to stand in front of me and restrained my wrists in his hands.

Rome trailed a hand down my bare back slowly. "I understand why you were scared, but you have to trust us, baby girl. We're here for you, no matter what."

Hunt and Gabe had taken up positions on either side of the couch, their eyes fixated on me. I could feel the intensity of their gaze, and it only made me more nervous but also turned on.

Rome leaned forward, his hand resting on the center of my back to push my breasts into the back of the lounge. "And that doesn't mean you can just dismiss us when things get tough, baby girl. We're a team, and we need to work through things together."

And with that, he stood back up and I felt his hands on my hips, pulling my ass upwards and back towards him. "Are you ready for your punishment, baby girl?"

Chapter 35

Alexis

I took a deep breath, steeling myself for what was to come. "Yes, Sir. I'm ready."

"Good girl," he praised, "Start counting for me baby girl and remember the rules, no cumming without permission. Use your colors if you need to."

I hear the slap of his hand against my ass. It takes a moment for the pain to actually reach my mind. It was harder than anything he has done before. It was sharp and the sting from it hurt. It felt like a live flame licking at my ass cheek where his fingers now softly smoothed over the skin.

"One." I breathed out.

Rome spanked me again, his hand connecting with my skin sending a jolt of pain through my body, but I also felt an intense heat building between my legs. I couldn't help but moan and whimper, my body betraying me.

"Two," I counted, my voice shaking as I braced myself for the next impact. Rome's hand came down hard again, and I cried out. my body shook from the force of it. But even as the pain reverberated through me, I couldn't help the way my pussy clenched in response.

"Three," I gasped, feeling the tears starting to leak down my face. Rome's hand continued to rain down on me, each blow harder than the last. But even as my body writhed under his touch, I knew that I was exactly where I wanted to be.

"Four," I moaned, my body beginning to shake with a combination of pain and pleasure. Rome's hand was everywhere, slapping my ass and stroking my skin, and I felt like I was on fire.

"Five," I whimpered, the pleasure was now starting to outweigh the pain. I couldn't help the way my body responded to Rome's touch, the way I longed for more.

"That's it, baby girl," Rome growled, his voice low and husky. "Take it like a good girl. You know you deserve this, don't you?"

"Yes, Sir," I gasped, my body writhing under his touch. "I deserve it. I need it."

"Good," Rome said, delivering another hard smack to my ass. "Because we're not done yet. You're going to count for me, baby girl, all the way to ten."

I moaned at the thought, my body already quivering with anticipation. I knew that the punishment was far from over, but I also knew that I couldn't wait to feel Rome's hand on my ass again.

Rome continued to spank me, the pain and pleasure mingling together until I couldn't distinguish between them. My body was on fire, and I was gasping and moaning with each strike of his hand.

"Six," I managed to get out, my voice hoarse with desire. Hunt and Gabe had moved closer, their hands trailing over my skin as Rome continued to punish me. Colt's eyes were fixed on me, watching my every move as he held my wrists in a firm grip.

"Seven," I cried out, my body shaking with every blow. Rome's hand was relentless, and I could feel the heat building between my legs with each strike.

"Eight," I whimpered. But even as the pain intensified, I couldn't help the way my body responded to the men around me. I could feel their eyes on me, their hands caressing my skin, and it only made me more aroused.

"Nine," I gasped, my body on the verge of exploding. I could feel the tension building in my core, and I knew that it wouldn't take much to get me over the edge.

"Good girl," Rome growled, delivering one final, hard smack to my ass. "Now ask for what you want, baby girl. Tell us what you need."

I moaned, feeling my body on the verge of release. "Please, Sir," I begged, my voice barely above a whisper. "Please let me cum. Please."

The men chuckled, their hands trailing over my skin as I waited for the response. Finally, Rome leaned down over me from behind and whispered in my ear.

"Cum for us, baby girl," he murmured, before he landed a sharp slap to my pussy that I felt in my clit. My body exploded in a wave of pleasure, and I cried out as I came, my body shaking and quivering under the touch of the men around me.

The pleasure was intense, and I felt like I was flying. I could feel the men around me, their hands on my body, their breath hot against my skin. It was almost too much to handle, but I couldn't get enough.

As the pleasure subsided, I laid there panting, my body still twitching from the aftershocks. The men were still surrounding me, their hands and mouths exploring my body as I basked in the glow of my orgasm.

Rome's hands smoothed softly over the burning flesh of my ass.

"That was so fucking hot," Hunt murmured, his lips trailing over my skin.

"I loved watching you take your punishment like a good girl," Gabe added, his hand slipping between my thighs to stroke my sensitive clit.

Colt was still holding my wrists, his eyes fixed on me with a hunger that made my body hum with desire. "You were such a good girl for us," he said, his voice thick and husky with arousal.

I moaned at his words, feeling my arousal building again. I wanted more, needed more of their touch, their attention. "Please," I whispered, arching my back and pressing myself back towards Rome. "I need more."

Hunt's hands found my breasts again, squeezing and teasing my nipples until I was gasping for breath. Gabe's fingers were still moving expertly over my clit, driving me closer and closer to the edge.

Colt leaned in to kiss me, his tongue tangling with mine as he held my wrists tighter.

"You want more, princess?" he growled against my lips. "Tell us what you want."

I moaned, my body writhing with need. "I want all of you," I panted. "I want your cocks, I want your cum, I want to feel all of you inside me for days."

"Then it's a good thing we are nowhere near finished with you, princess."

All hands disappeared from me as the men all shedded their clothes, Colt moving to join the others in front of the couch as Rome helped me stand up.

I watched hungrily as they revealed their muscular bodies, their cocks already hard and throbbing.

Colt stepped forward, his hand wrapping around my neck as he leaned in close. "You're ours, princess. We're going to make you scream and beg for more."

I whimpered at his words, feeling a rush of excitement course through me.

"But first, I think I need a reminder of how appreciative you are of us, princess. Get on your knees," Colt growled, letting go of my neck.

I didn't hesitate to obey, dropping to my knees on the soft carpet in front of them.

Colt's hand tangled in my hair as he pulled me closer to him. "Open your mouth, princess. Show us how much you love our cocks."

I eagerly obeyed, parting my lips and taking him into my mouth, feeling the weight of him as he filled me completely. The other men stepped forward, offering their own cocks for me to take, and I moaned with pleasure as I became fully surrounded by them.

Their cocks were all so close so I reached out to stroke them one by one, feeling their heat and hardness in my hand.

"Such a good girl," Hunt groaned.

I took turns licking and sucking on each of them, savoring the taste and feel of them in my mouth, my tongue playing with Rome's and then Gabe's piercings.

"Look at you," Gabe said, his voice rough with desire. "Taking us all in like the dirty girl you are."

I moaned around the cock in my mouth, the vibration sending shivers of pleasure through me. I could feel their eyes on me, watching as I worked my mouth over each of them.

When Colt's turn came again, he pushed my head down onto his cock, thrusting deep into my mouth. I choked slightly at the sudden movement, but he didn't let up, fucking my mouth with long, deep strokes.

I could feel myself getting wetter with each passing moment, desperate for more. I wanted them to take me, use me, make me theirs in every possible way. And from the way they were all looking at me, it was clear they wanted the same thing.

Colt pulled back, his cock glistening with my saliva as he looked down at me. "You're so fucking beautiful like this, princess," he said, his voice low and rough.

The others murmured in agreement, their eyes filled with hunger as they watched me worship their cocks.

It wasn't enough. I wanted them inside me, filling me up completely, and I was pretty sure they knew it too.

"Please," I begged, looking up at Colt with pleading eyes. "I need you inside me."

He smirked down at me, his hand gripping his cock tightly. "Beg for it, princess."

I didn't hesitate, my voice coming out in a desperate moan. "Please, please fuck me. I need it so fucking badly. I need you all to use me like you own me. Make me yours. Make me scream."

Colt flicked a look to Hunt who quickly disappeared as Gabe dropped to his own knees beside me.

"Look at me," Colt demanded, his eyes blazing with intensity.

I obeyed, meeting his gaze and feeling a shiver run down my spine at the raw desire I saw there.

"You're ours," he said, his voice low and possessive. "All ours."

I moaned softly in response, feeling my body responding to his possessive energy.

"Say it," he growled.

"I'm yours," I said, my voice barely above a whisper.

"That's right," he said, leaning down to kiss me fiercely, thrusting his tongue into my mouth to tangle with mine.

Gabe's hands started roaming over my body as Colt kissed me, touching me everywhere, sending jolts of pleasure through me.

"You love being our good girl, don't you?" he asked, nipping at my earlobe.

"Yes," I gasped as Colt pulled away from my mouth and stepped back, feeling my arousal building with each touch.

"Good," Gabe said, gripping my neck and pulling me closer to him. "Because we're going to use you until you can't take anymore."

I whimpered in response, knowing that I wanted nothing more than to be at their mercy.

"Say it again," he demanded, his eyes dark with lust.

"I'm yours," I repeated, feeling his grip tighten.

"That's fucking right," he said, "You're fucking ours. You will always be ours. You belong to us. This mouth is ours. This body is ours. This baby is ours. This pussy and ass are ours. You. Are. Ours."

I moaned at his possessive words, feeling my arousal building with each passing moment. I knew that I wanted nothing more than to be completely owned by them.

"You love it when we own you, don't you?" he asked, his hand slipping between my thighs to find my wetness.

"Yes," I gasped, my body arching towards his touch.

"That's it," he growled, rubbing circles over my clit. "You're such a dirty girl for us."

I couldn't hold back a moan as he continued to touch me, my body on fire with need.

"Look at you," he said, leaning in to kiss me fiercely. "All wet and needy for us."

I nodded, unable to speak as he continued to tease me.

"We're going to take you so hard," he said, his breath hot against my ear. "You'll never forget who you belong to."

I shuddered at his words, my body craving their touch.

"Are you ready for us?" he asked, his eyes burning with desire.

"Yes," I moaned, my voice barely above a whisper.

"Good," he said, pulling me closer to him. "Because we're going to fuck you until you can't walk straight."

Chapter 36

Alexis

Gabe's mouth moved down my neck and made its way to bite and lick at my nipples, his tongue piercing flicking over them. Rome stepped back up to my other side, his fingers threading into my hair to take a fist full to move my head to bring his cock back to my lips.

"Open up, baby girl." Rome demanded at the same time as Gabe bit my nipple hard, making my mouth open on a gasp and allowing Rome to shove his cock straight down my throat.

I choked a little at the sudden intrusion, but the feeling quickly turned into pleasure as I relaxed my throat muscles and allowed Rome to slowly fuck my mouth, my tongue flicking and swirling around the piercings along his cock. Gabe's mouth moved down my body, leaving a trail of kisses and bites. I could feel the cold metal of his piercings pressing against my skin with each kiss, until he reached my wet and aching pussy.

He laid down on his back and then dragged me over his body until I was hovering above him. "Sit this pretty pussy on my face, dirty girl."

I must have been lowering myself too slowly because he grabbed my thighs and pulled me down onto his face. He started to lick and suck at my clit, rubbing his piercing over and over against me, sending waves of pleasure through me as Rome thrust into my mouth.

He buried his face more forcefully between my legs and began to eat me out with a fierce hunger, his tongue delving deep inside me before swirling around my clit, the solid cold metal in his mouth hitting me in all the right places. I moaned around Rome's cock, my body trembling with pleasure.

"Fuck, you taste amazing," Gabe groaned, his fingers digging into my hips as he devoured me. "You're so wet for us already."

I moaned again around Rome's cock, rubbing my tongue along his tip and then slowly down each piercing, feeling my body building toward an orgasm. He groaned in response and his thrusts into my mouth grew more urgent, his fingers tightening in my hair as he fucked my mouth harder. The metal piercings clicked against my teeth every few thrusts as I swallowed around him. "You're such a good girl for us," he growled, his eyes dark with desire.

I saw Hunt return out of the corner of my eye bringing pillows and a bottle of lube. My pussy throbbed at the sight. After he threw them onto the ground close to us, he stood back with Colt where they both watched with hungry eyes, stroking their own cocks.

I felt the weight of Gabe's tongue piercing as he flicked it over my clit, driving me closer and closer to the edge. I arched my back further as I rode his face, grinding my pussy against his mouth as I sucked on Rome's cock with all my might. I changed the angle of my head to take Rome further into my throat. The sight of Colt and Hunt stroking themselves while watching us only added to the intensity of the moment.

I could feel the pressure building as Gabe's tongue expertly flicked and circled my clit, driving me closer and closer to the edge. Rome's thrusts became harder and faster, pushing deep into my throat with each movement. I could feel my own spit spilling from my mouth with each of his thrusts, dripping down my chin and onto my chest.

I wanted them all inside me, every inch of me filled with their hard cocks. I could feel my body trembling with need as my orgasm approached, and I knew I couldn't hold back any longer.

"Please... Please fuck me," I mumbled around Rome's cock when he allowed me room to breathe, my body writhing with pleasure, before he thrust his cock back into my throat.

"Cum one more time, dirty girl, and we will give you what you want," Gabe growled before sucking my clit back into his mouth and biting down.

I cried out in pleasure as my orgasm ripped through me, my body shaking and convulsing on top of Gabe's face. He continued to lap at my pussy as I came down from my high, his piercing scraping along my sensitive clit. Rome pulled out of my mouth with a groan, wiping along my chin with his thumb before shoving it into my mouth and then dragging it back out along my bottom lip.

Gabe pulled me down his body until I was straddling his waist, his hands immediately went to my hips, pulling me directly onto his cock. I moaned loudly as he filled me up, my body still humming from my earlier orgasm. His thrusts were slow and deliberate, his eyes locked onto mine as he took in my every reaction. "That's it, beautiful," he groaned. "Take my cock deep inside you."

Meanwhile, Hunt had moved closer and was now fisting himself just inches away from my face. I leaned forward, taking him into my mouth and sucking him eagerly, my body craving more pleasure.

Colt came over and knelt behind me, his hands roaming over my ass as he guided me to move with Gabe's thrusts. He leaned in and whispered in my ear, his voice husky with desire. "You look so fucking hot taking his cock, princess. And you're going to take all of us, one by one."

Hunt's hands were now on my head, guiding me as I sucked him deep into my mouth. "Fuck, your mouth feels amazing, sweetheart," he moaned. "I can't wait to feel you tighten around my cock when I fuck you again."

I moaned loudly in response, my body responding to his words and the pleasure coursing through me. Gabe's thrusts became harder and faster, and I felt myself building towards another orgasm.

Just as I was about to come again, Gabe pulled out of me, leaving me hovering and empty until the orgasm retreated.

Colt pushed me forward slightly and he rubbed his hard cock against my pussy from behind. "You want this, don't you? You want all of us, filling you up and making you cum over and over again," he whispered in my ear, his breath hot against my skin.

"Yes, please, fuck me," I begged, unable to resist the over- whelming desire coursing through my body.

"Good girl," he said, before plunging his cock deep inside me in one swift motion. I cried out in pleasure as he started to thrust hard and fast. I gasped at the sudden change, allowing Hunt to thrust deeper into my throat, but soon found myself adjusting to Colt's size and rocking my hips against him.

Colt's hands gripped my hips, pulling me back onto his cock with each thrust. His pace was fast and rough, and I could feel the pleasure building once again inside me. Hunt's cock pushed into my throat with each thrust, and I could feel his body tensing up as he got closer to his own release.

I reached up with my hands and gripped Hunt's hips, pulling him deeper as Colt's thrusts became harder and faster. The sensation was overwhelming, and I felt like I was on the brink of exploding with pleasure.

Suddenly, both Hunt and Colt pulled out of me, leaving me panting and gasping for air. Rome came to stand on Hunt's other side and Hunt used the grip he had on my hair to direct me back over to Rome's cock. At the same time Gabe once again pushed his cock deep into my pussy.

I eagerly took Rome into my mouth, savoring the taste and feel of him, my tongue rubbing against his piercings. I could feel Gabe's cock deep inside me, filling me up, the piercing at the end of his cock scraping against me, as he started to thrust harder. The combination of Rome's cock in my mouth and Gabe's in my pussy had me moaning uncontrollably.

Hunt grabbed my hair again and pulled my head back as he watched Rome's cock continue to thrust into my mouth. He wrapped his hand around my throat and squeezed gently, tightening it around Rome's cock until I'm sure he could feel each time it slid down my throat. "That's it, sweetheart, take him all the way down. You look so fucking hot with his cock in your mouth," he groaned.

Gabe leaned up, whispering in my ear, "You're doing so good for us, taking all our cocks like a good girl."

I moaned loudly, feeling so wanted and desired by all of them. Rome's hands were on my head, guiding me as I took him deeper and deeper, feeling his throbbing length in my mouth. Gabe's hands were gripping my hips tightly, pulling me onto his cock as he thrust faster, his words of encouragement spurring me on.

Hunt leaned in, his hot breath on my neck as he whispered, "You're such a good little dirty girl for us, taking all our cocks so fucking well. Look at you, so beautiful and willing for us."

I moaned again, my body writhing with pleasure as I was filled from both ends. The feeling of their hard cocks inside me, the taste of Rome in my mouth, and the sound of their dirty words and moans mixing together was overwhelming and intoxicating.

Once again I was left empty and on the edge of coming as Rome pulled out of my mouth and Gabe lifted me off his cock, leaving me gasping for more. Before I could even be sad about not cumming, Colt thrust his fingers inside me, hooking them to rub and thrust hard against my G-spot and at the same time Gabe started rubbing my clit.

"Oh, fuck," I cried out, feeling the intense pleasure shoot through me as Colt and Gabe worked me over with their fingers. "Yes, keep going, don't stop," I begged, my body writhing with need.

Gabe growled, "You like that, dirty girl? You love being filled up and finger-fucked like this?"

I shuddered in response, unable to form words as the pleasure consumed me. Gabe's fingers worked my clit with expert precision, while Colt thrust his fingers hard inside me, sending electric shocks of pleasure through my body.

I moaned, feeling the edge of a cliff fast approaching. "Yes, yes, yes!" I cried out.

Colt chuckled darkly, "You're such a good girl for us, aren't you? You can't get enough of what we do to you."

I gasped as he curled his fingers inside me again, hitting my sweet spot with every thrust. "Yes, yes, I'm your dirty girl," I moaned, the words coming out without thought as I lost myself in the pleasure they were giving me.

Gabe's voice was low and husky in my ear, "That's it, dirty girl. Cum all over our fingers."

I cried out as the pleasure exploded inside me, my body convulsing as I came hard. Colt and Gabe continued to work me over, drawing out every last tremor and wave of pleasure until I collapsed in a boneless heap.

"We aren't even close to being done yet, princess." Colt chuckled as he reached around and shoved his wet fingers into my panting mouth. He lined himself up to my still pulsing pussy and thrust hard inside me again.

I moaned around his fingers as he began to move inside me. His thrusts were hard and so very deep, filling me up completely with each stroke.

I desperately clung to Gabe below me, my nails digging into his chest as I rocked my hips in time with Colt's thrusts.

I heard the sound of the lube as Hunt poured some into Gabe's hand before it disappeared between us. My mind came online enough to be confused at the angle.

But then Colt stopped moving and Gabe pressed his cock to where Colt was already buried inside me.

Oh my fucking god.

I felt stretched beyond my limits as Gabe slowly pushed into my pussy alongside Colt.

Holy. Fuck.

I knew I wanted them to destroy my pussy, but I hadn't meant literally.

Chapter 37

Alexis

The moan I let out around Colt's fingers was obscene.

Colt's voice was low and gravelly as he spoke, his breath hot against my ear. "You like that, don't you, princess? Two big cocks filling you up at the same time."

I whimpered in response, unable to form words as the sensations overwhelmed me.

Colt withdrew his fingers from my mouth to wrap his hand tightly around my throat while his other hand gripped my hip tightly. Gabe began to thrust into me from below before Colt started moving too, matching Gabe's rhythm. The sensation was intense, and I moaned uncontrollably as they both filled me completely.

"Fuck, you feel amazing," Colt growled, his grip on my throat tightening just enough to send shivers down my spine. "We're gonna make you come so hard, princess. You're gonna scream for us."

I could barely hold on as they both fucked me relentlessly, my body being pushed to its limits with every thrust.

"Oh, fuck, you feel so good," Gabe growled, "I could fuck you all night long."

I could only moan in response, my body writhing between them as they moved in perfect sync. Colt's fingers found their way to my clit, and he began to rub me in tight circles.

Colt's grip on my throat tightened as he spoke again. "You're such a good girl, taking both of us so well." His words sent shivers down my spine as I felt the pleasure building inside me.

Gabe's hands were on my hips, pulling me down onto him with each thrust. I could feel his cock rubbing against Colt's as they both moved inside me. The sensation was almost too much to bear, and I was grateful for Colt's hand around my throat, giving me something to focus on besides the overwhelming pleasure.

The room was filled with the sound of our bodies slapping together and our moans of ecstasy. I was lost in the sensation of being completely filled by these men, my body completely surrendered to their desires.

I could feel the sweat glistening on my skin and the heat radiating from our bodies as we moved together in perfect harmony.

As Colt continued to thrust into me, his grip on my throat becoming tighter, I felt the familiar tightening in my stomach. "I'm gonna cum," I gasped out, barely able to get the words out.

"Fuck, I'm close," Gabe groaned, his movements becoming more erratic as he chased his own release.

Colt's hand tightened around my throat, and he leaned down to whisper in my ear. "You're gonna take every last drop from us, princess."

My pussy started to clench down tightly on their cocks, their movements starting to falter.

Colt's movements became more frantic as he felt my body start to convulse around him. "Cum for us, princess," he growled. "Cum all over our cocks." And with that, I exploded, my orgasm hitting me like a freight train. I screamed as wave after wave of pleasure crashed over me, my body shaking with the force of it.

As I rode the waves of my orgasm, I felt Colt and Gabe both thrusting into me hard and fast, chasing their own release. The sensation of their cocks pulsing inside me was enough to send me over the edge once again. My body convulsed as I came, my muscles clenching around them and squeezing every last drop of cum from their cocks.

Colt collapsed on top of me, his body heaving with exhaustion. He slowly pulled out of my pussy, pulling a whimper from me before he helped lift me off Gabe's cock and onto my knees on the floor between Gabe's legs.

His cock is still semi hard and slick with our combined cum. "Clean up your mess, dirty girl."

Gabe groaned loudly as I took him into my mouth, tasting the remnants of our earlier activities. I swirled my tongue around his length, tasting both him and Colt along with myself, savoring the mixture of flavors.

I hummed around him and felt him twitch in my mouth as he groaned again.

Then a tongue licked my pussy from my clit to my ass and I gasped, releasing Gabe from my mouth and allowing him to slide out from under me.

My pussy was so sensitive from Colt and Gabe. Rome groaned into my pussy as his tongue swirled around my clit before he buried it inside me. I gasped and pushed back towards him and he smacked a hand against my already tender ass.

"That's it, baby girl, take it," Rome growled, his tongue delving deeper inside me.

I moaned at his words, my body still humming from the multiple orgasms I just experienced. I could feel the wetness between my legs, evidence of just how much I loved being used by them.

I put my head down and moaned as Rome's tongue continued to work its magic on my pussy. My hips moved with his every stroke, pushing back against his mouth.

"Fuck, Rome," I panted. "Your tongue feels so good. I want you to fuck me with it."

Rome chuckled against my wetness, his fingers digging into my thighs. "Is that what my baby girl wants? To feel my tongue deep inside her tight little pussy?"

"Yes," I gasped. "I want you to make me come again. I need you to make me scream."

Rome chuckled and thrusted his tongue deep inside me. I groaned, my body arching towards Rome's talented mouth. I could feel my orgasm building again, my body ready to explode once more.

But just as I was about to come, Rome pulled away, leaving me hanging on the edge. I whimpered in protest, but he just chuckled and stood up. "You're not done yet, baby girl," he said, dragging me up to my feet.

He moved us over to the couch where he laid down along the length of it with his head resting on the arm. He pulled me over his body to straddle his waist, fisting his hard cock and running it against my pussy.

I moaned at the contact, feeling his hot length and all his piercings sliding between my wet folds. "Please, Rome, I need you inside me," I begged, grinding against him.

He smirked up at me, his hands gripping my hips tightly. "You're so fucking needy, baby girl. You want my cock that badly?"

I nodded eagerly, unable to form words as I rubbed against him. He chuckled and teased me for a few more moments before finally sliding his cock into me, filling me up completely.

I gasped at the sensation of his piercings against me, my body still sensitive from the earlier orgasms. He started thrusting up into me, his pace slow and steady, building me up again. "That's it, baby girl," he grunted. "Take my cock, make it your own."

I moaned loudly, my body rocking against him with each thrust. "Yes, Rome, your cock feels so good," I whimpered, my hands digging into his shoulders.

He picked up the pace, his thrusts becoming harder and faster, his hands gripping my ass tightly.

I felt another orgasm building with each of his thrusts until I was teetering on the edge again. Rome stopped moving and gripped the back of my neck to drag my lips to his in a deep and dirty kiss. His tongue thrusting into my mouth.

The feeling of lube gliding down my ass startled me but Rome only tightened his hold on me.

"Relax, sweetheart," Hunt whispered against my ear. "We're going to take care of you."

I trusted them completely and surrendered myself to the pleasure as his finger circled my tight entrance before pushing inside. My body tensed momentarily before relaxing around him.

Rome's mouth moved from my lips to my neck as Hunt added another finger, scissoring them inside me and stretching me out.

I moaned as the pleasure mixed with a hint of pain, my body adjusting to the stretch. "Yes, fuck, just like that," I panted, pushing back against his fingers. "I want both of your cocks inside me, now."

Rome chuckled darkly against my skin. "You want to be filled up, baby girl? You want us to fuck you at the same time?"

I nodded eagerly, my body trembling with anticipation. Hunt added a third finger, making me gasp and whimper at the delicious ache.

"Please," I begged, my voice barely above a whisper. "I need it, I need you both."

Without a word, Hunt withdrew his fingers and positioned himself at my entrance. Slowly, he pushed the head of his cock inside me, taking his time as he stretched me out even further. I moaned at the fullness, my hands gripping onto the arm of the couch tightly as Hunt slowly thrust deeper inside me.

"Rome, I can feel your fucking piercings," Hunt groaned, his hips meeting mine with each slow thrust.

I could feel Rome's lips curve into a smirk as they trailed down my collarbone while Hunt continued to move his cock inside of me. His pace was agonizingly slow at first, but as my body adjusted to the new sensation, he began to pick up the pace.

Rome started thrusting into my pussy again, his pace just as deep and slow as Hunt's.

I was completely filled, their cocks stretching me in all the right ways. I moaned loudly as they moved together inside me, their bodies syncing up as they fucked me.

"Fuck, baby girl, you feel so good," Rome groaned, his hands gripping my hips tightly.

Hunt's hands were on my breasts, squeezing and teasing my nipples as he thrust into me.

My body was on fire, my mind consumed with pleasure.

"Yes, fuck me," I moaned, my hips rocking between the two of them.

Hunt gripped my breasts tightly as he picked up the pace, his cock slamming into me harder and faster. I could feel my body tightening around them, my orgasm building once more.

The sound of our skin slapping together filled the room as they pounded into me, each thrust pushing me closer and closer to the edge.

My body was aching with need, craving their touch and their cocks. Rome's hands were gripping my hips tightly, pulling me down onto his cock with each of his thrusts.

"You like that, baby girl?" he grunted, his breath hot against my ear.

I moaned loudly, my body responding eagerly to his touch. "Yes, please, fuck me harder," I begged, my voice desperate with need.

He didn't need to be asked twice. With a fierce growl, he picked up the pace, his thrusts becoming harder and faster. I could feel the heat building inside me again, my body ready to explode with pleasure.

Hunt's hands squeezed my breasts, his fingers digging into my skin as he pulled me back onto his cock. "You feel so fucking good, sweetheart," he moaned, his breath hot against my neck.

I could feel the tension building inside me, my body vibrating with the need to cum. "Please, I need to cum," I whimpered, my hips rocking between them.

Hunt pulled my body back towards him using his grip on my breast so I was sitting more upright, changing the angle of them inside of me. Colt and Gabe stepped up to the lounge beside me, their cocks hard and throbbing again and I moaned at the sight of them.

I reached out and gripped both of them in my hands taking over for them by stroking along their cocks and gripping their bases. I leaned towards them as Hunt and Rome continued to thrust into me from below and licked along the base of one and then the other.

Colt and Gabe groaned in pleasure as I continued to stroke and lick them, while Hunt and Rome's thrusts became harder and faster. My body was being used for their pleasure, and I loved it.

Hunt's grip on my breast tightened even more, and I knew I was going to have bruises in the morning, but the pain only added to my pleasure.

Colt and Gabe took turns thrusting into my mouth as I continued to stroke them, licking and sucking them eagerly. I felt my body building towards an intense climax, my mind consumed by the pleasure and sensation of being filled from all sides.

Hunt's thrusts became even more frenzied, his hips slapping against my ass with a deliciously dirty sound. "You like that, sweetheart? You like being fucked hard by all of us?"

"Fuck, yes!" I responded huskily.

Rome's hands were on my hips, his grip tight as he slammed into me with increasing force. "You're so tight," he growled, "I can feel every inch of you squeezing around me."

Colt and Gabe groaned in pleasure as I continued to lick and suck on each of their cocks, taking them as far as I could down my throat before moving between them. I squeezed and stroked with my hand what I couldn't have buried in my mouth. I could feel Hunt and Rome's hands on my hips as they held me in place, their cocks filling me up completely.

"Fuck, you're so hot," Colt moaned as I took him deeper into my mouth, sucking and licking with abandon.

Gabe's fingers tangled in my hair as he pulled me closer to him, his cock twitching in my hand as I stroked him harder and faster. "Yeah, that's it, just like that," he groaned, "I'm so fucking close."

I could feel myself on the brink of orgasm, the pleasure building to an almost unbearable intensity. Hunt's grip on my breasts was painfully tight as he drove into me harder and faster, his breath coming in ragged gasps. "You're gonna cum for us, sweetheart," he growled, "you're gonna cum so hard for all of us."

Rome's thrusts became even more urgent, his hips slamming into me with a force that made me cry out in pleasure. "Cum, baby girl," he grunted, "cum for us."

Colt and Gabe's cocks were throbbing in my hands as they both reached the edge of their own climaxes. "Fuck, I'm gonna cum," Colt groaned, his fingers digging into my hair as he thrust into my mouth.

Gabe's grip tightened in my hair also as he pushed himself over the edge, his hips bucking as he spilled his hot cum all over my hand. I felt Hunt and Rome tense up behind me, their cocks pulsing as they both came hard, filling me up completely.

I screamed out in pleasure as my own orgasm ripped through me, the sensation so intense that I saw stars behind my closed eyes.

We collapsed in a heap on the couch, panting and sweating, our bodies intertwined in a tangle of limbs. "That was fucking amazing," Hunt murmured, his hand still lazily caressing my breast.

I grinned up at him, feeling a sense of satisfaction wash over me. "Yeah," I agreed, "it really was."

Chapter 38

Alexis

It was the night of the Gala, and as I slipped into the stunning dress Gabe and Hunt picked out, I couldn't help but feel like the luckiest girl in the world. I put on makeup and even managed to curl my hair using the supplies that all mysteriously appeared in the bathroom attached to my room. My guess was Gabe and Hunt once again.

I felt like a completely different person. I felt confident, beautiful, and loved.

Looking at myself in the mirror when I had finished getting ready was also like looking at a completely different person. It felt odd to not have a gun on me for once.

A month ago, if someone had told me that this would be my life, I would have asked if they were insane. I could never have imagined all those weeks ago that I would be in love with four men and be pregnant with their baby.

As I walked out of my room, I saw Gabe, Hunt, Colt, and Rome waiting for me in the foyer. Their eyes lit up when they saw me, and I couldn't help but blush at their attention.

Seeing them in their formal wear I almost couldn't believe that they were mine.

Each of them were dressed in their formal wear, looking as stunning as ever. Colt was wearing a classic black tuxedo, with a crisp white shirt and a black bow tie. Hunt had opted for a navy blue suit, paired with a light blue dress shirt and a patterned tie that perfectly complemented his piercing blue eyes. Gabe had gone for a slightly more casual look, with a dark gray suit and a black dress shirt, with the top button undone. Rome, on the other hand, had chosen a deep burgundy velvet blazer, paired with black pants and a crisp white dress shirt.

As I made my way down the stairs, the four men's eyes were fixed on me, and I could feel my heart race with anticipation. They all looked so handsome, but in different ways. I couldn't help but feel lucky to have them in my life.

Hunt stepped forward and took my hand, pressing a soft kiss to the back of it. "You look absolutely stunning," he murmured, his eyes sparkling with affection.

Gabe wrapped an arm around my waist, pulling me close to him. "I think we're going to be the envy of everyone at the Gala tonight," he whispered in my ear, his breath hot against my skin.

Colt leaned in and kissed me softly, his hand cupping my cheek. "You take my breath away," he whispered before stepping back to admire me from a distance.

Rome took my other hand, twirling me around to get a better look. "You are the most beautiful woman I've ever seen," he said, his voice full of awe and admiration.

I felt a wave of love wash over me as I looked into their eyes. These men, who had become such an important part of my life, loved me and accepted me for who I was. Even though the situation might seem unconventional to some, it felt right to me. As we made our way to the Gala, I knew that I was exactly where I was meant to be. By their sides.

Colt presented me with a large black box, holding it for me while I removed the lid and folded back the black tissue paper.

The masquerade mask that rested within was stunning. It was made in shades of brown and green and my heart squeezed upon realizing that they got it to match my eyes. It also complemented the beautiful green of the dress.

I smiled at Colt and reached up to kiss him, grateful for the thoughtful gesture. "Thank you," I whispered against his lips.

I moved to take the mask out of the box, but Rome beat me to it, lifting it by the ribbons and helping me secure it in place.

He turned me and leaned down to kiss me, his hands cupping my face as he looked into my eyes. "We love you," he said, his voice soft and full of emotion. "You're ours, and we'll always take care of you."

Tears pricked at the corners of my eyes as I looked at him, feeling overwhelmed by their love and devotion. "I love you all too," I said, my voice trembling with emotion. "And I know you'll take care of me and our baby."

Gabe pulled me into a group hug, kissing the top of my head. "Let's go make an entrance," he said, grinning at the others.

When we arrived at the gala, I was blown away by the extravagant decorations and the number of people in attendance.

As we walked into the grand ballroom, I couldn't help but feel a thrill of excitement. The room was filled with people, all dressed in their finest attire and wearing stunning masquerade masks. The chandeliers sparkled overhead, casting a warm glow over the room. Music floated through the air, played by a live orchestra on a stage at the far end of the room.

We moved through the crowd, mingling with guests and enjoying the delicious food and drinks that were being passed around. Everywhere we went, we attracted attention. People whispered and stared, clearly curious about the four handsome men and the woman on their arm.

I didn't care about the whispers or the stares. I was happy to be with my men, feeling their love and support surrounding me. As the night wore on, we danced and laughed and enjoyed each other's company, lost in our own little world. Any time I looked into their eyes, I knew that I found my home.

I was dancing to a slow song with one of the charity benefactors that Colt had introduced me to when I heard someone ask to cut in. Thinking it was one of my guys I moved into their arms automatically. Only to look into a pair of dark familiar eyes.

"Hello, Fiore Mio." Dominick said with a smirk.

My breath caught in my chest, and I went to step backwards only for him to tighten his grip on me.

"I wouldn't do that if I were you," he said, his voice low and dangerous. "I've missed you. It's been too long since we've been together."

I tried to pull away from him again, but he held me firmly. "How did you know I would be here?" I snarled at him.

"I told you before, no matter where you go or what you do, I will always find you." He smirked again, his finger slid softly down the back of my neck. "I'm just accepting the invitation you sent me to come get you myself."

I was so stupid. Of course it was that simple. Of course he had done something despicable. Of course he would put a tracker inside me.

I honestly should have known he was just that sadistic, but the thought had never occurred to me.

I looked around the room, but I couldn't see any of my men.

Dominick let out a low chuckle, his grip tightening even more. "I saw that you've got yourself some new friends," he said, "Your guard dogs are currently indisposed and they won't protect you from me."

I growled at his dismissal of them though worry flooded me for their safety. "They aren't guard dogs. They love me and I love them."

He tilted his head and raised his brow condescendingly. "Is that what you think? They are just using that pretty pussy until they get sick of it. Really, I should have known you were nothing but a dirty whore, throwing that cunt at anyone with a cock."

His words rolled over me and right back off. Nothing he could say would ever make me feel anything other than loved by my men. "Awww, don't slut shame, it's pathetic."

The humor fell away from his face, realizing his words weren't affecting me the way he wanted. With a growl he spun me around, and I felt the barrel of a gun pressed to my side. "I think it's time we took our leave."

My heart raced as I felt the cold metal of the gun against my skin. I knew that Dominick was capable of anything, and that he wouldn't hesitate to hurt me or anyone else to get what he wanted. I tried to stay calm and think of a way out of this situation.

"I'm not going anywhere with you," I said firmly, trying to keep my voice steady. "Let me go, Dominick."

He pressed the gun harder into my side, making me wince. "Don't make this harder than it needs to be, Fiore Mio," he said, his breath hot on my neck. "You belong to me, remember?"

As if on cue, I heard the sound of glass breaking followed by a loud commotion coming from the entrance to the ballroom. In the chaos, Dominick dragged me at gunpoint towards the back of the ballroom and down a hallway.

Chapter 39

Alexis

He shoved me roughly into a room, slamming the door behind us.

I stumbled and fell onto the floor, but quickly got up and backed away from Dominick, who still had the gun pointed at me. My heart was pounding in my chest and my mind was racing, trying to come up with a plan to escape.

"Who was that at the entrance?" I asked, hoping to distract him.

He sneered at me. "Just some idiots trying to play the hero. It won't do them any good."

I noticed that he was distracted for a moment, his attention on the door. It was a small opening, but it was enough for me to make a move. I lunged towards him, knocking the gun out of his hand and sending it flying across the room.

I went to scramble after it but he grabbed a handful of my hair and yanked me backwards. I let out a growl as my head was jerked back and my scalp burned.

I kicked out with my foot, thankful for the splits in the fabric of my dress. I landed a kick to his knee, and he stumbled backwards. I took advantage of the moment and made a run for the door, but he caught me by the arm and pulled me back.

"You're not getting away from me that easily," he growled.

He swung me around until my back slammed into the wall, knocking the air out of me. He was on me in seconds, his hand wrapping firmly around my throat.

I was dazed momentarily.

"Stop struggling, Fiore Mio," he snarled, his grip tightening. "You're only making this harder on yourself."

I gasped for air, my vision starting to blur. I knew I was in trouble, but I refused to give up.

Suddenly, I heard a loud crash from outside the room, followed by shouting and the sound of fists hitting flesh. I heard one of my men shouting my name, and I knew they had come to rescue me.

But then, did I actually need them to?

I kicked out and he managed to avoid my kick this time, but the kick was just a distraction for my punch under his arm forcing him to release me immediately. I stumbled to the side, gasping for air and trying to catch my breath.

Dominick recovered quickly and charged towards me, throwing a punch at my face. I ducked, barely avoiding his fist and landed a hard punch to his stomach. He grunted in pain and staggered backward a step.

He chuckled as he looked at me. "You're no match for me, Fiore Mio. Don't bother trying to fight me. You were only ever a pretty little whore to hang on my arm. Just come along now like a good little bitch."

The banging on the door had grown louder, shaking the entire wall, but the door held firm. I could hear them shouting my name.

I shook my head at him. "You're forgetting something Nick. It's been two years since we were together. I'm no longer the girl you left to die. That's boss bitch to you now."

I refused to show any fear, and instead, I circled him, looking for an opening. He was bigger and stronger than me, but I was faster and more agile. I could use that to my advantage.

He made the first move, lunging towards me. I dodged the hit he aimed at my head and landed a punch to his jaw. He stumbled backward, but quickly regained his balance and charged towards me again.

I grabbed a chair nearby and swung it at him. It hit him on the shoulder, but he brushed it off as if it was nothing.

I continued to circle him, searching for a weakness. Then, I saw it. A knife was strapped under his arm. The same knife he used to taunt and cut me.

I feigned a punch toward his face, causing him to raise his arms in defense. Then, I kicked his leg, causing him to lose balance. I grabbed the knife and held it out in front of me.

He chucked again. "I'm going to enjoy breaking you."

I didn't let his words intimidate me. Instead, I held the knife tightly and waited for him to make his move. He lunged towards me again, but this time, I was ready. I sidestepped him and slashed the knife across his arm, causing him to howl in pain and stumble backward.

Blood oozed from the wound, but he didn't seem to care. He charged towards me again, I ducked under his punch and stabbed the knife deep into his stomach before pulling it back out. He fell to his knees, gasping for air and clutching his stomach.

I stood over him, panting heavily, but feeling victorious. I looked down at him, feeling a mixture of anger and disgust. "You were never going to win, Nick," I said. "You lost the moment you tried to kill me. You know that saying, what doesn't kill you makes you stronger. You never broke me, and now you never will."

With a final gasp, Dominick slumped to the ground, motionless. I stood there for a moment, catching my breath and processing what had just happened.

He was finally dead. He could never hurt me or my family again.

I heard the door finally break open behind me, coming completely off the frame from the sound of it, and turned to see my men rushing in. They quickly assessed the situation, and rushed over to wrap their arms around me.

Colt framed my face gently with his hands. "Are you ok, princess? We were so scared when we couldn't get in here, security took our guns from us."

I nodded, still in shock from what had just happened. "I'm okay," I said, my voice trembling slightly. "It's over now."

He pulled me into a tight hug, and I felt the weight of everything that had happened over the past few months come crashing down on me. Tears streamed down my face as I finally allowed myself to let go of all the fear and trauma that had been building up inside of me.

My men led me out of the building, and I was greeted by a sea of flashing lights and sirens. The police had arrived, and they quickly took control of the situation. I gave a statement to the detectives while sitting in the back of an ambulance, explaining what had happened and how Dominick had escaped prison, hunted me down and attacked me. The detectives assured me that they would take care of everything, and that I didn't need to worry.

As the adrenaline started to wear off, I began to feel the pain of the cuts and bruises on my body. The paramedics were trying to do their jobs of helping me around the hovering presence of my men, but when one of them brushed a hand against my neck the memory of Nick's words came screaming back into my mind.

I freaked out.

"Get it out, get it out!" I screamed, grabbing at the back of my neck. "Nick implanted a tracker in me, you have to get it out!"

The paramedics hesitated, unsure of what to do. I could see the fear in their eyes as they looked to my men for guidance.

"Get the kit," Colt barked, his voice taking on a dangerous edge. "We'll take care of it ourselves."

Gabe nodded in agreement and quickly retrieved a medical kit from inside the ambulance. My men gathered around me protectively as Colt and Gabe began to work on removing the tracker. I could feel their intense concentration as they worked, their movements precise and calculated.

I squeezed my eyes shut and bit down hard on my lip to keep from screaming as I felt the sharp blade of a scalpel against my skin. It felt like an eternity before I heard Colt's triumphant shout of "Got it!"

My men quickly disposed of the tracker, and I breathed a sigh of relief.. The final weight of Nick's presence lifted from my mind.

As the adrenaline began to wear off, I could feel the pain and exhaustion settling in. Gabe took over and started to clean and dress my other wounds, completely disregarding the paramedics now.

Eventually, the officers finished taking statements, and I was allowed to leave. Colt helped me into the back of our car, and I leaned my head back against the seat, trying to process everything that had happened.

It was finally over. Dominick was dead, and I was safe. But the scars he had left behind would never fully heal. I knew I would never forget what had happened, but I also knew that I was strong enough to move forward.

I closed my eyes and felt a sense of freedom and relief wash over me. The weight of my past had finally been lifted, and I was ready to move on with my life.

I didn't know what the future held for me, but I knew that with these men by my side, I would be fine.

Epilogue

7.5 MONTHS LATER

Pleasure rippled through me as Rome rubbed circles on my clit, he licked up my jawline before nibbling at my ear. "You going to be my good girl?"

I tugged gently against the restraints holding me to the wall with a moan.

He had been reluctant to start this session given how close I was to my due date, but it hadn't taken too much convincing in the end.

I nodded, feeling the heat building between my legs. "Yes, Sir," I whispered, my voice sounding breathy.

He chuckled darkly, his fingers working me harder and faster. "That's it, baby girl. Let go for me."

I was lost in the pleasure, my body arching against him as I felt my orgasm building. Just as I was about to fall over the edge, a sharp pain shot through my lower abdomen.

I grunted at the pain, and then I felt a rush of fluid between my legs.

And it certainly wasn't cum.

"Pineapple." I gasped.

Rome's eyes widened in alarm as he pulled back, his fingers stilling on my clit. "What's wrong, baby girl?"

I took a deep breath, trying to steady myself as another wave of pain hit me. "My water just broke. It feels like a pineapple is trying to come out of me," I gasped out.

Rome's expression turned to one of panic as he quickly untied me from the wall. "Shit, we need to get you to the hospital."

He shouted for the others who came racing in moments later. At Rome's rushed explanation, they all moved with both the efficiency of an elite team and the panic of expectant fathers.

Gabe quickly cleaned me up while Colt pulled my dress back on over my naked body. Hunt went to retrieve my go bag and called ahead to the private hospital to let them know.

I was still panting, trying to catch my breath as the reality of the situation sank in. I was going to have a baby. I looked up at Rome, who was holding me close, his hand resting on my belly.

"Everything is going to be okay," he whispered to me, his voice thick with emotion. "We're going to get you to the hospital and you're going to have a beautiful, healthy baby."

I nodded, tears stinging at the corners of my eyes. I was scared, but I knew that Rome was right. With these men by my side, I could get through anything. We had already proven it so many times. Even so, a small part of my heart was sad to know my parents would not be here for the birth of their grandchild.

We had decided together as a family that our lives were still too dangerous for me to come back from the dead.

As we made our way to the hospital, the pain in my abdomen grew more intense and frequent. I clung to Gabe and Hunt's hands, squeezing them tight with every contraction.

When we finally arrived, the medical team sprang into action, wheeling me into the labor and delivery unit.

After what felt like hours of pushing, and many threats of multiple castrations, I finally heard the cry of my baby as she was born into the world. The tears flowed freely down my face as I looked down at her, taking in her tiny features and the sound of her cries.

Colt leaned down to place a gentle kiss on my forehead before he turned to look at our daughter. His eyes were filled with wonder and amazement as he took her in. "She's beautiful," he whispered.

Rome placed a gentle kiss against my head. "I'm so proud of you, baby girl. She's so perfect."

I smiled up at him, feeling overwhelmed with emotion.

Hunt and Gabe both leaned in to give me a kiss on the cheek before turning their attention to our new addition.

As the medical team took care of me and our newborn, I looked around at the faces of the men who had become my family. They all looked exhausted, but there was a sense of contentment and joy on their faces that I knew mirrored my own.

After a few moments, Hunt came over to me, holding out his arms for the baby. "Can I hold her?" he asked softly.

I nodded, passing our daughter over to him with care. He cradled her gently in his arms, a look of pure adoration on his face as he gazed down at her.

"She's so small," he murmured. "And so perfect."

Gabe and Rome each took turns holding the baby and marveled at her tiny features. Our little girl was healthy and perfect in every way, and we were already completely smitten with her.

It was in that moment, surrounded by the men I loved and our new addition to the family, that I knew I had everything I could ever need. The love and support of these amazing men, and the beautiful little girl we had brought into the world, made everything else pale in comparison.

I leaned back against Colt, feeling his arms wrap around me in a comforting embrace. As I looked around at my family, I knew that we had been through so much together, but we had come out the other side stronger than ever.

Hunt turned to me with a smile. "So, are you going to tell us what name you decided on? You have been very secretive about it."

I smiled, feeling a sense of pride and excitement as I looked down at my little girl. "Her name is Chrysalis," I said softly.

The room was silent for a moment before Rome spoke up. "Chrysalis?" he repeated a hint of confusion in his voice.

I nodded, feeling a rush of emotion as I explained. "A chrysalis is the birthplace of a butterfly," I said. "It's where the transformation happens, where something beautiful is created out of darkness and struggle."

There was a moment of silence as my words sunk in, and then Colt spoke up. "That's beautiful," he said, his voice filled with emotion. "Just like our little girl."

I smiled, feeling a sense of gratitude for these men who had become my family. "I wanted her name to represent the journey we've all been on, the struggles we've faced and overcome together," I said. "And I wanted it to represent the beauty that can come out of even the darkest moments."

The room was silent again, and I looked around at each of the men in turn, feeling overwhelmed with emotion. "She's a beautiful piece of all of us," I said. "Created in the midst of darkness, but surrounded by love and light."

There were tears in Colt's eyes as he pulled me closer, and I knew that he understood exactly what I meant. We had all been through so much together, but at that moment, it was all worth it. We had a beautiful little girl to show for it, and a bond that would never be broken.

I smiled, feeling a sense of contentment and joy wash over me. At that moment, I knew that our family was complete and that we had everything we could ever need. The love of these amazing men, and our beautiful daughter, were all I could ever ask for.

3 Months Later

I ran away.

Admittedly, it was with Gabe to go on a field trip that was planned, plus we left our daughter with her other fathers who were completely smitten and wrapped around her tiny little finger.

The gentle buzz of the tattoo gun had become like background noise.

I answered my phone as it rang, seeing that it was Ashley calling. "Hey girl, what's up?" I said, answering with a smile.

"Just wanted to check in on you, make sure you're doing okay, and how is my gorgeous niece?" Ash replied.

"I'm hanging in there, and she is still gorgeous," I said with a chuckle, grateful for her concern. "How about you? Everything good on your end?"

"I might have run away again," she admitted, her voice low.

"Again?" I asked, surprised.

"It's not like I can't be found," she scoffed.

"You're such a brat," I said, laughing.

"I know," Ashley said, sounding unrepentant.

"Just promise me you won't do anything too crazy, okay?" I said.

"I promise," Ashley said, laughing. "But I can't make any promises about staying out of trouble."

We both laughed.

"Plant a smooch on my niece's cheek and a bruise on my brother's shin," she giggled before hanging up, leaving me with a grin on my face.

The tattoo artist was just finishing up the tattoo as I thought about my baby girl. We had decided not to find out who she belonged to because as far as we were concerned she belonged to all of us.

But I could tell, even at only three months old, because she had Colt's beautiful green eyes and dark hair.

But she belonged to all of us. She was our miracle and our gift. Born from the love that we shared right from the start, we would raise her together as a family.

I felt Gabe's hand squeeze mine as the tattoo artist finished up, he had already finished his tattoo which was our daughter's name over his heart, right next to the tattoo he already got of my name.

"All done," he said with a smile, showing me the mirror so I could see the tattoo.

Across my ribs where before I had scars from Dominick cutting into me was now a cluster of five large blue butterflies with a single smaller one further up near my heart.

People forget the changes that a butterfly has to go through. The struggle. They have to learn to crawl before they can fly. They have to leave one life behind in order to start a new one. And they cannot see their own beauty while the rest of the world can.

"They're perfect," I breathed.

"They're beautiful," Gabe said, looking at the tattoo with admiration. "Just like you."

I smiled at him, feeling content and at peace. Despite everything we had been through, we had made it through to the other side stronger than ever. And we had a beautiful baby girl to show for it.

As we left the tattoo parlor and walked hand in hand back to our car, I couldn't help but feel grateful for everything that had led us to this moment. The pain, the fear, the uncertainty - it had all been worth it to have this family that we created.

And as I looked up at the sky, watching the sun slowly set behind the buildings, I knew that no matter what the future held, we would face it together, as a family.

Author's Note

I hope that you enjoyed the conclusion of the Shattered Safety duet and Lexi and the guys' story.

First off, thank you to my husband and my mum for always supporting me and putting up with my random obsessive personality that gets me totally lost in my writing, etc. I am hoping that you don't get to read this line considering the contents of the book but if you do read this please do not let me know so I don't die of mortification.

Thank you to Sarah and Jenny (AKA my Awesome Alpha Team) for your constant encouragement and support and for reading random chapters at a time for me.

Huge shoutout to my writing bestie Diana Long, who let me use words from her book for the library scene. If you haven't read her book Rhapsody of the Sea (Sons of Poseidon Book 1) you need to!

A big thanks to Ash for being my own personal cheer-leader.

And to Jessica from Book Dragon Designs for your amazing work.

Thank you also to all my betas and to my ARC team, for helping a baby author like me.

And lastly thank you to you, my readers, for once again taking a chance on me out of all the amazing authors out there, I completely appreciate it and you.

xx

Maree Rose

About the Author

Maree is a baby author who although she has been writing most of her life, never thought she would ever get something published, which is now why she published this herself. She has always been an avid reader since a young age after roaming through book exchanges with her mum when she was just starting to read serious big girl books.

Maree lives on the East Coast of Australia with her wonderful husband, her son and her two gorgeous squishy british bulldogs.

When she is not writing she is working in a financial career (for something completely different to the creative side) or she is working on her photography (which is just as hot as her books).

www.ingramcontent.com/pod-product-compliance
Lightning Source LLC
Chambersburg PA
CBHW072351110726
47909CB00003B/671